MISTLETOE MAGIC

A HOLIDAY ROMANCE NOVEL
BOOK 2

AMANDA SIEGRIST

McCord Family Novel

Protecting You

Trust in Love

Deserving You

Always Kind of Love

Finding You

Dare You to Love

Mona & Mason

The Paranormal Chronicles, Volume I

Perfect For You Novel

The Wrong Brother

The Right Time

The Easy Part

The Hard Choice

Psychic Love Novel

Exploding Love

Captured Love

Slaying Love Novel

Won't Let You Go

Doomed Love

Deadly Crazy

Evidence of Sin

Finding Redemption

Obsessed Hope

Short Stories

Paint By Murder

Follow Me, Sweet Darling

Sleighville Novel

Dashing Through the Fear

Here Comes Chaos

The Last Noel

Standalone Novel

The Danger with Love

Conquering Fear Novel

Co-written with Jane Blythe

Drowning in You

Out of the Darkness

Closing In

MERRY CHRISTMAS.

MAY YOUR DAYS AND NIGHTS BE FILLED WITH HOLIDAY CHEER!

1

————

HER BACK ACHED, her feet, her legs, her arms, hell, her fingers even tingled with unnecessary pain. Grabbing the plates from the countertop, she whisked through the kitchen double doors as if she had no aches or pains anywhere on her body. Because in her line of work, she needed to ignore it.

"Lunch rush over?"

"Sure is. Just cleaning up now." Theresa smiled at Bonzo as she tossed the dirty dishes into the sink filled to the rim with hot soapy water.

They had a nice ritual. She cleared everything up. He washed. Then she dried and put everything away. In between, of course, helping any customers that strolled into the diner as he continued to cook.

"Today lasted longer than normal."

Blowing out a heavy breath, she offered another smile. "You know how it is during the holidays. Stop making such good pies."

Bonzo winked. "Stop making such good coffee."

Laughing, she walked back to the front. He sure liked to

make jokes. Because that was the silliest one she ever heard. She made horrible coffee. Absolutely disgusting. He knew it. She knew it. Everybody knew it. Yet, they all came flocking in for her coffee. One of these days, she might actually make a good pot.

It's not as if she didn't try. She searched the Internet for the perfect way to make a pot of coffee that would put a smile on everyone's face.

Make sure to use the correct kind of water. She laughed when she saw that, wondering why the type of water would make a difference. But it did. It suggested filtered or bottled water for the best flavor, and on occasion, tap water was acceptable. And don't pour in cold water or the coffee won't be as strong, too hot and it'll burn and give off a bitter taste. She almost stopped searching just based on reading all the water facts.

Next, the ideal amount of scoops for the coffee grounds. One to two tablespoons of grounds to every six ounces of water. She made a big pot of coffee, so she tended to put in quite a few scoops. Messing with the amounts never made a difference. Each pot still tasted disgusting. Even to her.

Then there was the perfect filter. Bonzo bought filters in bulk from his food supplier, so she had no control over that. She figured Bonzo wouldn't steer her wrong in that department since he also waited for the day she would make a delicious pot of coffee.

And the last important detail she found was to thoroughly clean the coffee pot regularly. She did, like a maniac, making sure it sparkled like a twinkling diamond.

Even after all of her research, pouring over information from several different sites, her coffee-making skills still failed her horribly. Honestly, she figured the coffee pot just hated her because she watched Bonzo make it, doing exactly what she did, and it tasted delicious.

Whatever. Her coffee-making skills still had the diner hopping because people were always curious what it would taste like any particular day.

Shuffling back and forth on the floor, she cleared every table, wiping it down and rearranging everything just right. Not one person entered to interrupt her great pace. It was best if she worked fast because her body was ready to collapse into a big heap. The faster she went, the better chance she wouldn't faint from the aches.

The bell above the door rang with merry. Glancing up, her heart froze, then jumped into a dizzying pitter-patter rhythm that always happened when *he* walked in.

"Officer Crowl, good afternoon." She could only hope he couldn't hear her heart racing like a thousand wild horses.

"Afternoon, Theresa." He stopped before her, less than two feet of counter space separating them. "I'll have a cup of coffee."

He didn't smile or offer any other pleasantry. Straight and to the point. He always acted that way. To everyone, not just her. Which was why she never took offense at it or worried that he didn't like her.

Of course, she knew he didn't like her anyway, regardless of his lack of a smile. He hadn't been the same since his fiancé died over a year ago. A tragic car accident that shook their small town at the time. Cynthia had been the homecoming queen three years straight *and* the Mulberry Princess four years straight. Theresa never had the gumption or courage to enter the contest to be crowned the Mulberry Princess, the title given away every summer during the Fourth of July festival and picnic.

Cynthia had been the town sweetheart. Loved by everyone. Especially by Officer Crowl. They'd been the golden couple. He had been the star quarterback of the football team and almost went pro until he hurt his knee in a skiing accident in the off season of his junior year in college.

Theresa always had the worst crush on him, since ninth grade, and he didn't know she existed. Even now, she didn't think he really saw her. Just another waitress serving him a cup of coffee that would taste awful.

"Theresa? Can I get a cup of coffee?" His brows rose.

"Oh, yes, of course. My bad." She laughed nervously and turned around to the coffee pot. *You're an idiot.* Pouring the coffee quickly in a to-go cup, because he never stayed for his coffee, she realized she should've been more prepared for his arrival. He was like clockwork. Every day at two o'clock, right before his shift started, he came in for his coffee. She could only blame her tiredness.

Still feeling off-kilter, she turned back toward him, nearly dropping the coffee cup. His piercing brown eyes, almost black, looked at her with such intensity. Probably thinking what an imbecile she was, just standing there, staring at him moments before.

"One coffee." Another nervous laugh slipped out.

"Thanks." He tossed a five to the counter and took a sip. A wince crossed his face.

"That bad?"

He coughed. "Not at all. Have a good day."

"You, too." Yet her words were lost on him, as he was already halfway to the exit. Obviously, he couldn't get away fast enough. He always left her a decent tip, though.

Lame. That's what she was. Pining and wishing and hoping for a man that would never return her affection. Oh, well. She learned early on in life she didn't always get what she wanted and it was just best to move on.

The bell above the door rang again. She knew right then she'd be gaining five pounds.

"Lynn Duncan! I swear, if you're here dropping off more cookies, I'm gonna...gonna...become fat."

She laughed as Lynn set a container down in front of her, her eyes twinkling with mischief. "What, you don't like my cookies? I make them for the diner, not you specifically."

"Yeah, but they're soooo good and I can't resist." Theresa opened the container and snatched one, chomping down with delight. "Ugh! Can you seriously make them terrible, just once?"

Lynn took a seat, shaking her head as she laughed with her. "Elliot wouldn't like that."

"Me either."

"I wasn't going to bring another batch in until Friday, but then Mrs. Thompson stopped into the bakery and said you guys ran out, so I whipped out another batch today instead."

"Only you could whip out a batch of cookies and they taste like perfection."

"Thank you. How about some coffee before I pick up Laura from school?"

Cocking a brow, she smirked. "You sure? You know my coffee."

"Best coffee I've ever had."

"Now I know you're jesting." Theresa pointed a finger at her as she laughed, then turned around to get her a cup.

"Elliot loves your coffee, too."

"Chief Duncan is just too kind to say it tastes disgusting." Theresa set the cup of coffee before her.

"I saw Officer Crowl just left. He comes in every day for a cup." Lynn raised the cup to take a sip.

"I guess he's just being kind as well."

"Or..."

Wishful thinking. Please don't go there, Lynn.

"Does he have any clue you like him?"

Lynn must've interpreted her expression and decided to change tactics.

"I have no idea what you're talking about."

Taking another sip, Lynn looked like she was trying to choose her words carefully.

Theresa liked her. She met Elliot Duncan, Mulberry's Chief of Police, last Christmas, and it didn't take long for them to get engaged. A few months later, just as the flowers started to bloom, they were married. A few months after that, Lynn opened her own bakery two stores down from the diner. She made everything from breads to doughnuts to cookies to cakes to any sweet anyone asked of her. Bonzo, the owner of the Mulberry Diner, loved her cookies and asked her to supply the diner. She had become good friends with Lynn just from her weekly visits to drop off cookies.

"He's always so serious. I don't think I've ever seen him smile."

"He has the best smile." *When he used to display one.* Groaning, Theresa slumped her head to the counter to hide her embarrassment. "I didn't just say that."

"But you did."

Lifting her head, she saw Lynn's cheeks flush a bright red.

"I'm still in that honeymoon stage. I want everyone to be happy. Especially around Christmas."

"Have you finished shopping for Laura yet?"

And just like that, the conversation moved along. She didn't want to think about Officer Crowl, let alone talk about him. Distancing herself from him was crucial. Even when he came in to grab his coffee, she always addressed him as Officer Crowl instead of Aiden. It was easier. Way, way easier to control her crush on him and never let him know how she felt.

He was out of her reach. She accepted that. She didn't want to explain that to anyone else.

———

AIDEN SLAMMED his car door closed, taking another sip of coffee before putting it in the cup holder. He couldn't hold back another wince. Damn, the coffee was...bad. Not as bad as yesterday's batch, but still...bad.

He wondered if Theresa would ever get it right. Maybe. Maybe not. A bet was going on at the precinct for when, or if, she'd ever make a good cup. He threw twenty in the pot, saying she'd get it right by Christmas. Although, as he backed out of the parking spot, then took another sip, he figured he'd be losing twenty bucks.

Driving around, he waited impatiently for a call to come through the radio because it was always better for him to be occupied than his mind working in overdrive. Sitting at home, in the silence, the loneliness, all he did was think. Think about her. Think about regrets. Think about what was said before she walked out of the house. Thinking was the bane of his existence. Working was always better than time to himself to think.

Two hours later, no calls coming in, which was usual for their small town, he pulled into a spot outside the precinct. He decided he'd take a stroll up and down Main Street rather than get back into his car. He could use another cup of coffee. Last night had been—

Thinking again. Not good.

He stepped out of his vehicle. The cold wind bit into his cheeks.

"How's the day going so far, Officer Crowl?"

Aiden glanced to his right. "Just fine, Chief. A little slow, so I'd thought I'd get a refill of coffee."

"Not too bad today, huh?" Chief Duncan laughed. Aiden gave a slight tilt to his lips, the only indication he was amused by that as well.

He hadn't laughed or smiled in over a year. There wasn't much for him to laugh and smile about. Not when Cynthia was gone. Because of him.

"I know Lynn restocked the cookies today. You should grab one. They're delicious."

"I've no doubt." He waved goodbye as Chief Duncan headed for his truck, and most likely, home to his family.

He wanted to smile and feel happy for him, but even a simple emotion, like happiness for another person, was difficult on the best of days to conjure. He always wanted what Chief Duncan had. Now, he'd never get it. He wasn't worthy of it anymore.

Pulling open the diner door, the bell rang annoyingly in his ears. He saw an older couple in a booth eating the house special for the week, meat loaf and corn. In another booth, Councilman Jenkins sat with another guy he didn't recognize. He nodded at him, then searched for Theresa. He didn't see her anywhere on the floor. She must be in the back. Grabbing a seat at the counter, his fingers tapped a rhythmic pattern as he waited for her to come out.

Sitting still wasn't good. His thoughts roamed when he sat for too long.

The double doors swung open and Theresa's smiling face breached his thoughts before they could turn anywhere else.

"Officer Crowl, hello again."

"I need more coffee." He pushed his cup from earlier closer to the edge to her side of the counter. "Please."

He knew he could be standoffish to some people, especially people who didn't know him, but he could work on his manners a little. Her smile had dimmed at his words, at his lack of manners. He loved it when she smiled. Seeing it disappear wasn't something he'd wanted.

She had the brightest smile he'd ever seen. So large and consuming and infectious. Sometimes it made him want to smile in return, just because. Then Cynthia's face punched him in the gut and his frown went lower instead.

Theresa grabbed his cup and turned to the coffee pot.

"It was that delicious, was it?"

"Slow night." He coughed. What a dumb response, and an insult. "I enjoy your coffee." Her coffee might never taste good, but he would never intentionally offend her.

Swiveling toward him slowly, her smile was still there, just not shining within her eyes. "Didn't your mother tell you it's not nice to lie? I know how badly my coffee tastes."

He took the cup from her, his fingers grazing hers. A tingle of *something* zapped him. Something he hadn't felt in forever. Something he should try his damndest to ignore. Something he didn't want to feel. Something he didn't deserve to feel.

"I don't lie."

With that, he threw two bucks on the counter and left.

Yeah, she had the prettiest smile on the planet. It didn't matter. Nothing did. Not since he lost Cynthia.

"BE CAREFUL OUT THERE, girlie. It's cold out. I think it's about time you got a car."

She patted Bonzo's shoulder. "You know I enjoy walking. It's not too cold. I'll see you tomorrow."

The little bell above the door jangled merrily as she walked out. Pulling her scarf tighter around her neck, she dipped her chin lower as she made the small jaunt to her home. Well, small jaunt in her eyes. Some would agree, like Bonzo, that it was a long walk to make, especially in winter. Three blocks straight, then a right, another four blocks before she took a left, then five more blocks.

She lived at the end of the road in a small house that she rented from Mrs. Tanzia, a sweet older woman who moved up north to live with her children. The rent was cheap, and her son, whenever something went wrong, was quick to have someone come over and fix it. Most spots were safe in Mulberry, but like every town, it had its slightly run-down areas. Her house happened to be in that part of town. She wasn't ashamed of it, nor did she ever feel unsafe. Nothing new from her childhood either. She had lived in this part of town her entire life. It suited her just fine.

Twenty minutes later, she saw her house, welcoming the warmth that was soon to come. Most days she didn't mind walking. Today, well, it wasn't one of them. The brisk wind biting into her cheeks, mingled with her hands that couldn't stay warm even hidden in her coat pockets, confirmed how cold it truly was. And the soreness covering every inch of her body hadn't dissipated once. A nice hot bath to soak her bones would be one of the first things she did.

As she neared her front door, she couldn't hold back her groan.

"What a nice greeting from my sister." Her brother, James, stood up from lying on her stairs. "I need some cash."

"Hello to you, too."

"Didn't we just have those niceties. You know, where you

groaned at seeing me." He stepped down the two stairs, getting right in her face. "Just a little cash."

The strong smell of alcohol made her want to gag. Great. After her horrifying embarrassment with Officer Crowl, dealing with her drunk ass brother was not on her to-do list.

"I don't have any money for you. Get a job."

"You have a job. You have money."

"Go home, James." She started to go around him when he grabbed her wrist, yanking her back.

"Give me some damn money."

"For what, more booze?" Glancing at his hand wrapped tightly around her wrist, she tried to pull away. "Let me go."

The pressure increased. "I need some rent money."

"I know when you're lying. You smell like a damn brewery." Using as much strength as she had left, she tugged harder against his restraint, simultaneously pushing at his chest. She managed to break free and rushed to her door.

The handle twisted with ease, making her curse out loud at the fact he broke into her house. She opened the door quickly and slammed it shut just as fast, twisting the lock. The pounding started instantly.

"Let me in, Theresa! Just give me some damn money! I need it!"

Even though she flipped the lock, it was flimsy as hell. Holding her body against the door, she debated what to do. This wasn't the first time James had come around asking for money. She knew it wouldn't be the last. The first time he did it, she thought he actually needed help, giving him a little cash to tide him over. A few days later, she found out he spent it all at the bar. Giving in the first time had been her undoing. Now he thought she'd hand over money any time. No more. She worked hard for her money. He didn't do a damn thing but get into trouble and drink.

She had to change her locks twice already because James broke in by picking her locks, and then swiped her spare key she always thought she hid well enough. Apparently he did it again because she knew she locked her door this morning. She never forgot to lock her doors, especially living in the not-so-safe neighborhood. How many times would she have to change her locks? Better yet. How many times could she afford to?

The door shook as he pounded again. "You'll be sorry if I have to break down the door. Where'd you hide the money?"

Tears started to well up in her eyes. Why did her brother have to turn out like their deadbeat dad? The town drunk. Like father, like son.

She didn't always get to the bank to deposit her tips. Sometimes, she didn't make a whole lot to make a trip to the bank. It seemed easier to keep it at home, and she liked using cash instead of her credit card. Using her credit card was just a disaster waiting to happen.

She was going to have to start changing her routine, head to the bank to deposit her money before coming home. Thank goodness she hid her money well enough so he couldn't find it; surprisingly, since she never hid the spare key well enough. She learned her lesson on that, though. Her brother was a shifty one, and smart. She never underestimated him.

"Theresa!"

"Go away, James. I'm not giving you any money." Taking a deep breath, she hesitated. She didn't want to do it.

The pounding increased.

She had no choice.

"If you don't leave, I'll call the police."

"Yeah, do that." Pound. Pound. Pound. "I hope it's Officer

Crowl working. I'd love to tell him the pathetic way you pine over him." Pound. Pound. Pound. "Just a little cash to tide me over."

His voice held a hint of remorse. Just a hint. Then the pounding increased. She was more than a little worried he'd break through the door. He had never physically grabbed her before. Would he hurt her? Well, he *was* drunk. Fear swamped her for the first time dealing with her brother like this.

Digging in her purse, having difficulty locating her phone, she dumped everything on the floor. Her things scattered everywhere. Her phone slid across the floor, out of reach. A deep, fortifying breath escaped as she lunged forward, snatched her phone, then pressed her body back against the door.

Please, don't let Officer Crowl respond. Although, did it matter? It wouldn't be the first time he responded when her brother was drunk as a skunk and spouted how much she loved him. Officer Crowl never commented on it to her brother, or even her. She didn't exist to him, even when it was thrown right in his face.

She dialed nine-one-one.

Boy, what a great start to the holiday season.

2

AIDEN ALMOST JERKED the wheel into the ditch when he heard the address come through the radio. Her brother. Again.

After relaying with dispatch he was the closest one to respond, which was fine by him, he sped toward Theresa's house. He already felt horrible with the way he spoke to Theresa earlier. An apology was due. He needed to work on his manners and not act so abrupt with everyone, especially her. She was one of the sweetest women he knew.

Her brother was the worst kind of loser. He couldn't stand the jerk, always bothering Theresa, getting downright nasty with her. Yeah, he was more than happy to respond. He didn't like it when her brother gave her problems.

Less than five minutes later, he pulled to a roaring stop in front of her house. Her brother stood on the steps, banging on the door.

Stepping out of the vehicle, Aiden shouted, "Brennen, step away from the door."

He stopped banging on the door and turned toward him, laughing like a maniac. "Oh, look, Theresa, your knight in shining armor is here. Want me to see if he likes you as much as you like him?"

The dumbass was drunk. Great. He kind of asked for it. He wanted something to do besides thinking.

"It's time to leave, Brennen."

"That's Mr. Brennen to you, asshole." He spit at him.

Luckily, his aim was off; otherwise, his anger would've skyrocketed. Getting spit on was the worst. Truly disgusting. The call just went from a simple trespassing to an assault against an officer. Because yeah, he was going to be a dick and lock him up for spitting at him, regardless if it hit him or not.

"Put your hands behind your back. You're under arrest for assault."

"I didn't assault anyone. Get off my sister's property."

"You do realize she called us. You're also trespassing. Let's go, Brennen. Hands behind your back."

Just like that, the call went from a simple assault, that he was stretching to make, to an actual assault as Brennen jumped off the stairs and took a swing. Aiden was embarrassed to admit, even to himself, the move caught him off guard. Brennen's fist connected with his mouth and he staggered, almost pitching to the ground before he caught his footing. Then another fist came at him, but this time he managed to block the punch.

In a normal situation, Brennen was a strong guy. But drunk as he was, his reflexes were slower, making it easy for Aiden to take him to the ground. Now, getting the handcuffs on him might take a little work because he wouldn't stop resisting. He was debating his next move, quite tempted to throw his own sucker punch, because that's what the first one delivered to him was, when Officer Stockman appeared out of nowhere.

They had him handcuffed soon after.

"You mind taking him in for me. I..." He let his words trail off, essentially communicating he was still sorely tempted to beat the living shit out of Brennen for getting that punch in.

"No problem." Officer Stockman nodded to him. "Lip's still bleeding."

"Yeah, make sure to get assault on an officer, resisting arrest, drunk and disorderly, and trespassing."

"You got it." Officer Stockman dragged Brennen to his vehicle as he spouted vulgar obscenities the entire way. Aiden ignored every word.

He turned toward Theresa's house, the door still securely closed. Most people would've been standing outside, either shouting to add in more charges or screaming they didn't want him arrested. Theresa was never like most people. She never opened the door until they had her brother under control. Then she would come out and ask as nicely as possible if they would just remove him from her property. Not arrest him. It drove him nuts. She never wanted to press charges. She was just too damn nice.

Her generous spirit was one reason he liked her. Always so friendly. Always so happy. Always so beautiful.

Wait, what?

Sure, she had a beautiful smile, but that's it. Nothing more. He couldn't afford to think of anything else about her as beautiful. While he liked how kind she could be, he didn't like that she always let her brother get away with his behavior.

Knocking quietly on the door, he spoke in a soft voice. "Theresa? It's Officer Crowl. Can you open the door? He's gone."

The door swung open and his heart stopped beating.

The pain in her eyes almost had him pulling her into his arms to take it away. Then, just as swiftly, it disappeared as he effectively pushed those annoying emotions away. No good would come from feeling that way.

"Oh, my. He hit you. You're bleeding."

Fireworks exploded in an instant when she grabbed his hand and yanked him inside. There was nothing gentle in the way she pulled him down the hallway and into the living room. Maybe she thought he'd resist. Damn it, he would've if not for the way her touch was playing hell with his body.

The brief times they'd touched, just a little brush of fingers as she handed him a coffee, he felt it. That *something*. He couldn't describe what it was because he didn't like to think about it. Thinking was bad.

But right here and now, the way she grasped his hand, holding on with a firm grip, he couldn't ignore what that something was.

Desire.

He hated it.

Disengaging his hand from hers, almost rude-like, he took a step away from the couch where she wanted him to take a seat.

She looked puzzled. "I'm sorry. I didn't mean...have a seat. I'll go get a washcloth."

Before he could protest, she scurried away. His feet ached to run, to flee as fast as possible. Yet he stood immobile. Her soft touch still lingered on his palm.

No! It was all wrong. He shouldn't—couldn't—feel this way. He'd ruin her. Just like he ruined—

He squeezed his eyes shut as he tried to block his mind from any thought that would pull him down the rabbit hole. His dizzying thoughts jumbled into one big mess until his heart skipped a beat. Her hand touched him again. Popping open his eyes, he stared straight into her emerald green eyes, not missing the pain that was back. Before, her brother put it there. This time, he did it.

Her hand fell away from his shoulder, then her other hand hung between them with a wet washcloth. "For your lip. I can't believe he hit you."

"Yeah, he's not the brightest bulb on the Christmas tree." Aiden took the washcloth, careful not to touch any of her fingers. He couldn't handle anymore touching. "Did he hurt you?"

His gaze flicked to her wrist as she rubbed it furiously.

"No."

"Are you sure?"

"I don't lie."

He almost staggered back at the tone in her voice. He deserved that. Wiping his lip, unsure of what to say, if he should even say anything, he let the warm rag soothe the crack in his lip.

"What did he want?"

Wrapping her arms around herself, she shrugged. "What he always wants. Money. I told him no and to leave and he wouldn't listen. I didn't want to call the cops."

"You never do." He wanted to take a step closer. It took all his restraint to stay firmly where he stood. "It's a good thing you did. He's drunk. He could've hurt you."

"He's my brother. He'd never hurt me."

Aiden didn't respond. Not much he could say. Calling her a liar didn't seem right, but he heard the doubt in her voice. Hell, he doubted it himself. Her brother's drinking was getting steadily worse. He wouldn't put it past Brennen to lay a hand on his sister. And if he did, he'd answer to him. No one would ever hurt Theresa. Absolutely nobody.

Whoa!

Where did these protective feelings come from? One little touch from her and he wanted—

There he was thinking again. He thought he had perfected not letting his thoughts get carried away.

"You want to press charges, right?"

She bit her lip.

"Theresa...this isn't the first time and it won't be the last. Every time you call us, we come and make him leave without arresting him. He's not going to stop if you don't send a message. Because merely calling us isn't sending the right message." The warmth of the washcloth in his hand slowly disappeared as the temperature in the room chilled to an iceberg. If it was even warm to begin with. It normally wasn't when he was around. "Regardless, he'll be sitting on an assault charge."

"He has a problem. He needs help, not a jail cell."

"I know. But he always refuses help, so maybe a cell will give him time to reflect." He could've laughed at that statement. Reflecting about things never led to anything good. "It's up to you. Yes or no."

"I'll talk to him when he's sober. I'll get him some help. I don't...want to press charges."

His lips thinned into a tight line. Of course, it wasn't his call. If she didn't want to press charges, he wouldn't press the issue. Without her statement, the case wouldn't go very far. At least he could get him on the assault charge. The little punk needed to learn a lesson.

He glanced away, unable to stand the hurt in her eyes. He did nothing but be a jackass all the time, and no matter how much he didn't want to act that way, he couldn't stop it.

A Christmas tree stood in the corner of the room, close to the television. A sad looking tree. Not full and bristly like his parents always got every Christmas. Oh, and they went all out, venturing into the woods to pick the perfect tree, then his dad chopping it down like he was some sort of lumberjack when in reality he was an accountant.

The branches on the tree were small, sparse in some spots, and a tint of brown towards the back. Obviously Theresa was trying to hide that part, situating it against the wall with the hope people wouldn't notice.

Besides the sad, pitiful look, she had it decorated beautifully. Bright, colorful lights twinkled all around. Ornaments, from glass balls to homemade wooden crafts, hung from the thin branches. On the very top, an angel rested with grace and beauty. Most people had a star on top, his parents included. He had to admit, he liked the angel there instead. Something about the delicate angel spoke to him. Like it could see straight into his soul and wipe clean the pain and regret with one simple look.

"Nice tree."

She coughed, as if she was trying to hide a laugh. He whipped his gaze to hers. She thought he was being sarcastic, that he honestly didn't believe it looked nice. Because it was, puny as it appeared.

"It is a nice tree."

"Thank you." She turned her eyes away. "Are we done?"

"You don't have any popcorn strings on there."

"What?" She looked back at him confused.

He was a little confused himself. Why did he just say that?

"You know, stringing popcorn. It's a tradition in my family."

"Well, it's not in mine. I wouldn't know how to do it."

I could teach you. The words punctured his thoughts too quickly before he could stop himself. And so unwelcome.

He might think it, but he'd never say it out loud. It was for the best if he kept his distance.

"If you change your mind about pressing charges, let me know. I wish you would. He'll see the judge tomorrow for a bail hearing. Have a good night, Theresa."

He set the washcloth on the end of the couch and walked out. It wouldn't do well for him to think about Theresa in any manner other than how badly she made a pot of coffee. Anything else was unacceptable.

THERESA GRABBED the washcloth before it soaked into her couch. Not that she could brag about her couch, but still. It seemed like every time she spoke to Officer Crowl, it didn't go so well. And like the jerk her brother could be when he drank, he had to spout out words of her love to Officer Crowl, who still had the manners to ignore it. One of these times, she wished he'd just come out and say, "Why does your brother keep insisting you like me? You don't, right?" Then she could say, "Actually, I do." Then she could sink to the bottom of the floor where he could stomp all over her heart. Then she could move on with her life.

Of course, it would never happen. She was doomed to live with her secret, pining and hoping one of these days he'd see her as more than just the girl who made terrible coffee.

Glancing at her Christmas tree, she shut her eyes for a brief second, then swore out loud. "You idiot, Theresa. When will you learn?" Stalking to the tree, she yanked on the cord, unplugging it from the wall. She had left the tree plugged in while she wasn't home.

Like she had a bad habit of doing, she left it plugged in

last night before going to bed. She knew better than that. But she just loved seeing it lit, even if it wasn't the prettiest tree out there. Sometimes money could be scarce, especially when her brother came sniffing around and stole from her. She couldn't afford to be picky when it came to buying a tree.

On December first, every single year, she was at Jeff's Tree Lot to pick out her tree. She had it set up in the corner of the room, same spot every year, decorated and looking as beautiful as she could possibly make it. Sometimes she ached to purchase a tree the day right after Thanksgiving, but she had a ritual. December first. She wasn't going to change her routine no matter how much she wanted to. It was fun to go out searching for a tree, getting it home and decorating it as Christmas music swirled around the room with merry abandon. Bonzo was always sweet and transported it home for her.

She saw the way Bonzo looked at the tree she picked out this year. She even saw the look in his eyes that showed he wanted to buy her a better one. Of course, she stopped that suggestion before it even happened with one simple glare. Her tree might not be the prettiest, but it had character. That's what mattered to her. So what if it had a little brown mixed with the bright, vibrant green. It didn't mean the tree didn't have love to give. And by love, she meant, beauty. Every time she looked at the tree, all lit up in its glory, she saw nothing but beauty. Which was why she always forgot to unplug it. She hated when the lights went out.

But she knew a terrible habit when she saw one, and it was an accident waiting to happen. Thank goodness Officer Crowl didn't realize it had been plugged in the entire day. He probably thought she plugged it in when she got home.

She could already picture the look of disappointment and irritation on his face for doing something so stupid.

"Well, I am home now." She plugged the tree back in and smiled brightly. Much better.

It felt good to smile, especially after the incident with her brother. Sometimes he made it difficult to smile. He brought the trouble on himself tonight. She didn't like to think of him behind bars, waiting for bail, but there wasn't much she could do about it. He hit an officer. Not just any officer, but Officer Crowl, who didn't stand for behavior like that. A different officer might have given him a break, especially if she asked them to, but not Officer Crowl. He was by the book. On everything.

He had a point. Every time she called the police, which was always her last choice, she asked them to make him leave, not arrest him. Tonight, James scared her. He had never grabbed her before. Her father hadn't been an abusive man, just a raging alcoholic. But there had been times when a dangerous glint entered his eyes that made her think he wanted to hit something. Maybe one of them. James had that same nasty look tonight. She was better off not tempting the beast. He needed help. He may annoy, frustrate, and piss her off sometimes, but ultimately, he was her brother. She'd do everything in her power to get him help.

She'd pay his bail tomorrow and try to get him the help he desperately needed. Hopefully he didn't resist every step of the way. Knowing James, he would.

Her family wasn't that tight knit, or the best example of what a typical family looked like, but they were family. She couldn't leave her family hanging. Her mother would never forgive her if she left James in jail. Being the sole person in the family that made decent money regularly, she had the means to bail him out. Working in a diner didn't bring her tons of money, but it was better than what they did. Floating from deadbeat job to deadbeat job.

She made a light dinner, a simple turkey sandwich, and grabbed a bag of chips, plopping down on her couch. The silence was pleasant. Absorbing the beauty of her Christmas tree even lovelier. What would make it truly magical was some music. She grabbed her phone and hit play on her music app, and the wonderful melody of Christmas music filled the air. During the month of December, she never listened to anything other than holiday music, programming her music app so she didn't even have to search for the wonderful holiday sound. It just started to play.

She could describe Christmas in one simple word.

Magical.

No matter how aggravating life could be, she enjoyed Christmas and every little thing that came with it.

If only she didn't keep running into Officer Crowl and continue to make every situation worse with her words.

What did he think of her now?

3

THE MORNING RUSH had been crazy. The lunch rush even crazier. She finally had everything cleaned up, cleared away, and in the sink waiting for Bonzo to start washing. She'd been walking up and down the floor behind the counter, wiping it, rearranging menus and the condiments lining the counter, just waiting. And waiting.

He was late.

Officer Crowl had yet to step inside the diner for his daily coffee.

What did it mean?

Perhaps he was finally fed up with her, her family drama, and the things she said. He probably thought she was an idiot for not pressing charges against her brother—again. How many breaks should a person get? She had no clue. She just knew she didn't like to see her brother get in trouble, even if he deserved it.

Nothing too horrible was said between her and Officer Crowl last night, but apparently he didn't like her stance on not pressing charges.

That had to be the reason. He always came in for coffee. Always. What other explanation could there be?

The bell above the door rang merrily. Her heart pitter-pattered for about a second until she saw who it was. Attempting to hide her disappointment, she smiled at Lynn.

"You're so lucky your hands are empty. If you had more cookies for us, I would have...done something."

Lynn laughed as she took a seat on a stool. "The way they disappear so quickly around here, I might have to bring in more tomorrow. I wanted to talk to you about something. As you know from our conversation yesterday, I have almost all of Laura's presents bought for Christmas. I've never finished shopping this early before. It feels...amazing." Lynn laughed, the sound filling the diner with such happiness.

"Well, if I remember correctly, Chief Duncan and his dad spoiled her rotten last year. I imagine it's just as bad this year." Theresa smiled. She never had a Christmas where she got tons of presents, but her mother always managed to make it a beautiful time of year.

Lynn sighed. "You have no idea. I don't know how many times I can tell those two to settle down. I've since learned to just let them have their way. Especially Gregory. There is no stopping that man. He keeps saying the only thing he wants for Christmas is another grandchild."

Theresa's mouth opened in surprise as a little giggle escaped. "And will he be getting his wish?"

"Not in time for Christmas, no." Although Lynn's eyes sparkled with mischief. "I have a favor to ask you."

"Sure. How can I help?"

"I ran into your mom at the grocery store last week."

Theresa held her breath, wondering how that went. Her mother could be the utmost sweetest woman on Earth. Then in the next breath, hell on wheels. Her mother didn't drink like her brother and father did. But her mother didn't need alcohol to become a monster.

"And?"

"She was wearing the most beautiful beaded necklace. I asked her where she got it from and she said you made it."

Her heart, that had started to beat madly like a drummer going crazy, slowly dimmed to a steady beat. "Oh, yeah, it's something I do on occasion."

"Theresa," Lynn said, her eyes growing large, "do you really have no idea how beautiful that necklace is? You should be selling those left and right."

"Don't be silly. It's just something I do to pass the time." In truth, she had no life outside of work. Obviously Lynn was just being kind.

"Nonsense. They're gorgeous and I'd like to put in an order."

"For what?"

Lynn produced a gentle smile. "For you to make me some necklaces. Three of them. Two for Laura and one for Gabby. They'll be perfect for Christmas presents."

Whoa. She was being serious. "I don't think—"

"I'm not going to let you argue with me. I'll pay fifteen dollars a piece."

"Fifteen!" Now she knew Lynn was playing with her. "They're simple beaded necklaces. They are not worth fifteen a piece. And what happened to little miss gotta-save-my-money-in-any-way-I-can?"

"She's on vacation right now. I have a successful business and Elliot's slowly teaching me how to part with my money since I have money to spend now." Her laughter filled the room again with happiness. "And I imagine it takes time and energy to make those necklaces. Not to mention the supplies. I insist on paying fifteen dollars. Will you please make me three of them?" She pushed a sheet of paper across the counter. "Here's the color schemes I'd like."

"You're not going to let me say no, are you?"

Lynn shook her head as a bright smile lit her face.

"Fine. Give me a few days."

"Great! Thank you so much, Theresa. I better go get Laura now." With that, Lynn left.

Theresa grabbed the paper and glanced at it. She wanted one necklace blue and purple, one red and orange, and one all green. Easy enough. But fifteen dollars a piece? Really? Completely outrageous. Although, Lynn did have one thing right. It did take time to make them, especially when she worked with the tiny beads.

She made all sorts of necklaces, from simple ones with a few beads attached, to extravagant ones made out of all beads. Sometimes she dabbled in bracelets and earrings as well. It was something she had done since she was a child, occupying her time when she had nothing else to do, considering she didn't have a ton of friends growing up. It never occurred to her people would want to buy them.

A slow smile grew. It felt kind of wonderful that someone wanted to buy, not just one, but three. Of course it was Lynn who wanted to buy them. Lynn was one of the sweetest people she knew.

That's it. There was her answer.

Lynn was just being kind. She wanted to help out a friend. It hurt to think like that, but the truth hurt sometimes.

She pocketed the piece of paper and went back to wiping the counter down that didn't need it. She had to keep herself busy somehow. He was late for his coffee and she hated pondering why. Her body felt much better today, especially after she soaked in the bathtub for over an hour last night. The glass of wine might've helped as well.

The bell above the door rang.

Without looking up, she greeted the newcomer as she continued down the counter with light strokes.

"One cup of coffee...please."

Her head whipped up to the sultry voice she sometimes heard in her dreams. Officer Crowl looked like his normal unapproachable self. His chocolate brown eyes bore into her, almost stripping her bare. It unnerved her.

"Of course."

She set the rag down on the opposite counter and poured him a cup of coffee. Taking a fortifying breath, she turned around and set the coffee down in front of him.

"You bailed your brother out."

He said it with such accusation.

She had rushed to the precinct early this morning before her shift started and paid her brother's ridiculously high bail that probably set her back a month. Although, James promised to pay her back. That was as close to an apology as she would get for his behavior last night. When he was sober and needed something, he acted like the sweetest brother on the planet. He even promised to get help for his drinking. Since she needed to get to work, she couldn't make sure he went somewhere immediately to start the process.

"I did." She had nothing else to add. Her eyes shifted from his to the annoying sign on the front door that kept slipping down. "Excuse me."

She walked away and around the counter, passing Officer Crowl. She could sense him watching her as she grabbed the sign from the floor and tried to hang it one more time. The adorable Christmas magnets she used to keep it hanging obviously weren't strong enough to keep it up. This was close to the tenth time she had to rehang them today. Bonzo liked to have the daily special hanging on the door so people passing by could see it instead of everything written on a sign inside the diner. If they saw it before stepping inside, it might entice them to grab a bite to eat.

She found the holiday magnets at a garage sale this past summer. One was Rudolph, and the other, Santa Claus. They were adorable and so Christmassy she couldn't help but use them. Now she was thinking she'd have to grab some tape and hang the sign up the way she normally did.

Turning around, she jumped back, hitting the door. The paper fell once again. The magnets tumbled to the floor with a soft thump. Officer Crowl stood before her. Very closely. Too closely.

"Thanks for the coffee."

She wanted to step aside, but couldn't with a booth on each side of the door. She couldn't step forward because that would put her right into his arms. Although she wouldn't complain about that. By the look on his face, he wouldn't like it as much. Nothing but a scowl marred his face.

Then why did he insist on boxing her in? She could open the door and step outside to let him out. Or, he could step back and let her walk away.

She didn't say anything. He didn't move. They just stood there staring at each other.

Swallowing, she tried to think of something suave to say, or even something as dumb as "Can I get by?" She wiped her hands across her apron. The weird encounter was getting more awkward by the second.

She started to open her mouth to speak when his mouth swooped down and grazed her cheek. Then he brushed by her, his body almost flush with hers as he pushed the door open. Her feet still wouldn't move.

"What was that?"

He pointed above her. "Mistletoe." The door closed. He was gone.

She looked up, eyeing the mistletoe Bonzo hung a few days ago. Some people ignored it. Some, mostly couples, loved to stop and kiss each other. She'd never been kissed under any kind of beautiful mistletoe before. And the first time she was, it was on the cheek. How lame.

Did it mean something? That he liked her?

It had to mean something, even if it was a little lame. Why else would he kiss her? Half the time he barely tolerated her. But he kissed her on the cheek when he could've ignored the mistletoe. She forgot it hung above them, and she watched Bonzo hang it up. How could she forget when he clearly noticed it?

The situation went from weird to mystifying. So strange.

She picked up the paper again, slapping the magnets a little harder than necessary.

Maybe he was just playing a game with her. Wouldn't be the first time some jock played her for a fool.

Her steps slowed as she walked back behind the counter.

Well, that wasn't fair. They weren't in high school anymore. Even though Officer Crowl had been a jock, he'd never been one of them that made her feel worthless. If anything, he was indifferent, barely knew she existed back then.

Now he just acted weird. He seemed to like Christmas based on his comments last night. Maybe he felt compelled to kiss her under the mistletoe because that's what you did. People always kissed under mistletoe.

Of course that's why he did it. He felt obligated, not

because he wanted to. It was silly of her to think otherwise. She went back to wiping the counters that didn't need any more cleaning.

THERESA GRABBED her big jewelry box, or more like fishing box, from her bedroom closet and sat down in the middle of the living room. Years ago, before her dad started to drink heavily, he used to love to go fishing. He had a huge fishing box that held so many tackles that he almost couldn't close it. Eventually the alcohol took over, and he didn't even care about fishing and tossed his box with everything inside into the garbage. On a crazy impulse, she pulled it out, putting the fishing supplies in a separate box, and kept the fishing box for herself. She still had her dad's fishing gear in her closet. He'd probably never use the stuff again, but she couldn't find it in herself to throw it away.

She grabbed the supplies and laid them out in front of her. Luckily, she had the colors she needed for Lynn, but she did have to stop at Betty's Craft Corner before she came home today to grab some charms and a package of end connectors for the necklaces. She always liked to add a bit of whimsy on her pieces. With Laura and Gabby in mind, she bought two monkey charms, since Laura loved monkeys, and a beautiful rose charm for Gabby.

Lynn didn't specifically say what design she wanted, just specific colors. Without thinking about what she was doing, she set to work, hoping she created something they'd all love. Who knew? Maybe this was the beginning of a new adventure. She loved working at the diner, but when she really pondered her choices, she didn't think she wanted to work there for the rest of her life.

But where would she work? The diner was all she knew.

As she threaded bead after bead, the idea to create beautiful jewelry as a job grew. It was such a fanciful idea. She had no idea why she even thought she could make it possible. Theresa Brennen wasn't made for greatness. Just a simple diner girl who made shitty coffee.

Realizing she was working in silence, she snatched her phone, and with a few tap, tap, taps, Christmas music swirled around the room, lifting her spirits even more. Lifting her fanciful ideas to newer heights.

Why in the world couldn't she start a jewelry business? It couldn't hurt to try.

With a decision firmly in her mind, she worked steadily on the first necklace late into the night. By the time she went to bed, her mind still couldn't shut off from all the plans in her head.

Morning came too quickly, but part of that was her fault. She set her alarm a half hour earlier so she could work on Lynn's order before she left for work. Now that an idea was planted, she couldn't help but feel compelled to work on it. She was so enthused, she wanted more orders. Although now she was just getting ahead of herself. Would someone else really order anything from her? Maybe this was just Lynn being Lynn. Her wonderful nice self. Too nice sometimes.

Slumping against the couch, she sighed. *You're being ridiculous, Theresa.* Of course Lynn was just being overly kind. What was she thinking? Nobody else would want her amateur necklaces. All those plans she made last night were ridiculous.

Her eyes flew to her tree to lift her spirits because any time she looked at the beauty of it, her happiness level skyrocketed. She couldn't help but smile as the lights shimmered back at her.

"Oh, you idiot!"

She left the tree plugged in again last night. Jerking up from the floor, she yanked the plug out of the outlet. Why did she keep forgetting? She always remembered to keep it watered and from dying, but she frequently forgot to unplug it.

Stomping out of the living room, she decided to get ready for work. So much for feeling a little happiness before leaving.

When she reached the diner and prepared the coffee—that even made her cringe with disgust—her mood was so bad she wanted to slump to the floor and have a good cry.

"What's got your crank?"

Pausing outside the double doors before heading out to deliver two egg platter specials, she offered a simple smile. "That time of the month."

Bonzo chuckled. "Try again. This ain't that kind of pissiness. You've been acting funny this morning." His smile dimmed. "Something happen with your brother again?"

"No. I'm fine." She lifted the plates. "These will get cold if I don't deliver them."

She pushed through the doors before Bonzo could interrogate her some more. The plates settled down onto the booth table with a light tap even though she ached to slam them down. Her nerves were still rattled, and her anger swam on the surface. She couldn't even explain to herself why she felt this way. So ridiculous.

Maybe she could classify it as self-doubt. It shouldn't put her in such a cranky mood, though.

"Enjoy your breakfast, Mrs. Wayworth."

A bright smile echoed back. "Thank you so much."

She started to walk away.

"Oh, I meant to ask you something, Theresa. I spoke to Lynn yesterday."

She slowly turned around.

"She said you were making her a few necklaces for Christmas gifts. My sister lives in New York and is just so difficult to buy for. I love the idea of a necklace. Could you make me one as well?"

Holding back her dumbfounded look was impossible. Did Lynn do this on purpose? What was going on? Another order for her jewelry? She wasn't that good. Or was she?

"I shouldn't have asked. I know you work so hard at the diner every day. I still haven't figured out why Bonzo doesn't hire someone else to help." The way Mrs. Wayworth said it, she honestly thought Bonzo overworked her on purpose.

Not true, of course. He could afford to hire another person, but every time he thought about it and asked her, she said it was all good. And it was. They were never too busy that they couldn't handle it. If she ever needed time off or got sick, Bonzo's wife, Shelly, came in and covered for her. Her and Bonzo worked well together. They had a routine. Hiring someone else would disrupt that. Before she came along, his wife helped him. Then she got pregnant and wanted to stay at home with their twins, although she still worked on the weekends. The situation worked for them.

"I'd love to make you a necklace. They aren't fancy or anything. I'm no professional."

Mrs. Wayworth waved her hand. "Nonsense. I've seen expensive jewelry before, and honestly, half of that crap doesn't compare to the beauty you create. I've seen the stuff you've made. I love it." She pulled her wallet out of her purse and produced two twenties. "I'll take two, please. One red and one green. Can you have them done by Friday? I know that only gives you two days, but Christmas is in less than three weeks and I have to mail them to New York. Will that be a problem? Am I being too forward?" She pulled another twenty out. "To make it a rush order."

Wow. That was a lot of money. Too much.

"I can't accept that much. I can have them finished by Friday." She'd have to put Lynn's to the side, but she figured Lynn wouldn't mind and would understand the reasoning for it.

Mrs. Wayworth stood up and curled the money into her palm—all three twenties. "I insist. Consider part of it a tip for making such beauty."

"But I haven't made them yet. Maybe they'll come out looking like crap."

Mrs. Wayworth's hand tightened around hers. "Have more faith in yourself. Believe in the beauty you create." Her smile brightened as if rays of sunlight were shining upon it. "I'll stop by in the morning on Friday to pick them up."

"Thank you, Mrs. Wayworth. I won't disappoint you."

She laughed as she took her seat again. "Of course not. I have no doubt they'll turn out gorgeous." Picking up her fork, she wagged it in front of her. "You just wait and see. Once my sister opens her present, you'll have tons of orders. She knows lots of people."

Theresa walked away, her dreary mood lifting. She had another order, even if Lynn was behind it. But why? To what end? Just to be a nice friend? She didn't care. It was wonderful to know people liked her creations. Maybe her idea last night wasn't so farfetched.

As she walked back through the double doors to grab

another order that was complete, she decided it wasn't a horrible idea, but she wasn't ready to voice it to Bonzo yet.

Maybe she'd never be ready. That would take guts. Something she didn't think she had. Not enough, anyway.

4

THE LAST TWO days dragged by. Aiden hated when he had off. Chief Duncan knew if there was overtime available, he'd be the first to jump in line. Work always helped him more than sitting at home by himself, the silence eating him alive. Of course, overtime was rare.

For the first time, he missed not just work, but heading to the café for his usual coffee. On his days off, he never ventured to the café. Hell, he rarely ventured out of his house, even though he hated the loneliness.

Theresa was starting to invade his senses. He couldn't figure out how she did it. He had managed to keep his emotions in check since Cynthia died. Looking at another woman, let alone having dirty thoughts, was unacceptable. The last two days, he couldn't get Theresa out of his head, or the thought that he should've kissed her on the lips instead of a chaste kiss on the cheek.

What was that about?

He told her it was because of the mistletoe. Which was mostly true. He did kiss her because they had been standing under the mistletoe. He couldn't deny he also did it because he couldn't control the impulse. He *wanted* to kiss her. That was something he hadn't wanted to do in a long time. Too long, actually. He shouldn't have given in. Kissing her, even as innocent as it was, probably gave her the wrong idea. He wasn't looking for a relationship. Next time he stood under the mistletoe, there would be no kissing. Better yet, he'd never stand under one again.

It wasn't right. These feelings were wrong and unwelcome. It'd be in his best interest if he skipped going to the diner for his coffee. That way he wouldn't even be tempted to get Theresa under the mistletoe again and kiss her properly. On the lips with some tongue.

Yep, it'd be much better if he didn't go to the diner.

Yeah, and how did that work out for him last time? He lasted, what, thirty minutes, before he caved in and went to get his coffee. Pathetic.

It wasn't the coffee he craved. When he thought about it, which he tried his damndest not to do, he didn't think he ever went to the diner for just coffee. He went because he wanted—

Thinking shit like that wasn't helping. He knew better. He wouldn't do anything but cause her pain. That's all he was good for.

"Have a lovely day, Aiden."

His steps slowed as he neared the front door of the precinct and glanced at Daphne, who sat behind the front desk counter.

"Yep. You, too."

"Just one little smile. My Christmas gift from you."

"I don't do gifts, you know that, Daph." He winked. The closest thing he'd offer besides a smile. She asked every day for one, and he could never muster one up even to make her happy.

"One of these days..." She shook her finger at him as she laughed. "Oh, are you stumped on a gift for your mom? Because every year you rush at the last minute trying to figure out what present to get her."

That statement hurt. Daphne obviously tried to make it sound like every year meant every year for years, when in reality, it meant last year only. Every year before that, Cynthia handled the gifts. For everyone they knew. Not because he couldn't handle it but because she liked to control everything. She always thought she knew best.

So laughable. His mother never liked any of the gifts he gave her. Not that she ever voiced it, but he saw it in her eyes every time she opened them.

Not last year, though. He did have to scramble to grab a gift for her because his emotions had been haywire. He thought he had a better handle on everything this year, but he was obviously wrong. The strange feelings he had for Theresa were a prime example.

"It hasn't crossed my mind yet."

"Well, I have it on good authority that Theresa is finally taking orders to make necklaces for people. She makes such awesome jewelry. I don't know why she didn't start ages ago." Daphne flashed another sweet smile. "Anyhoos, I think your mother would love a necklace made by her. You should ask her to make you one. But I'd hurry. I hear she has quite a few orders to do already and she might get too busy to make any more."

Here he was trying not to think about her, and Daphne was throwing her right into his thoughts. Even worse, she was forcing him to go speak to her. Because damn it, his mother *would* like a necklace from her. A memory filtered in as he remembered a comment she made one time on the necklace Theresa was wearing when they all ate at the diner as a family.

"Thanks, Daph."

He left before she talked his ear off for the next hour, which was something Daphne excelled at. She loved to talk, no matter the topic of choice.

Pausing on the sidewalk, he glanced both ways. Right to the café? Left to his car? Making decisions sucked, yet he found his feet moving to the right. He always got a coffee and he'd be damned if his erratic thoughts about Theresa would sway him from doing what he always did.

The bell above the door jangled as he pulled it open and stepped inside. His eyes glossed to the mistletoe above.

Nope, damn it. No thinking about kissing.

He took a seat on a stool and waited patiently while Theresa helped a couple with a toddler at one of the booths to his left. He knew she worked from eight in the morning until five-thirty every day. Yet she never looked as tired as he imagined she was. Who wouldn't be rushing from table to table every day? The town might be small, but the café usually had steady business.

She turned, halting in her steps when she made eye contact with him. Did she feel the attraction between them as well? Or was the jerky movement more of a great-I-have-to-deal-with-him sort of halt?

Making her way behind the counter, she grabbed the coffee pot and a foam cup. Neither spoke. Not even polite pleasantries. He felt like a jerk for not saying hello, but the words were stuck in his throat. Why did that keep happening more and more with her? Each time he saw her, he just wanted to soak up her beauty and sweetness. He needed some of that in his life.

No, you don't. You don't deserve it.

She set the coffee cup in front of him and smiled. For once, he wanted to return the smile, but he stopped himself.

"There you go."

"Has your brother been bothering you lately?" Just like that, her smile disappeared. What was wrong with him? Where did that question come from? He *was* curious, especially since he didn't trust her brother, but he never intended to ask that question.

"My brother isn't your concern, Officer Crowl."

Ouch! She sure knew how to put him in his place.

He stood up and leaned forward, his mouth inches from hers. She froze, not moving away as he wanted her to. As she should. Talk about playing hell on his nerves. He wanted to close the distance and claim her lips.

"It is when you call the cops."

"Then I'll stop calling you—the cops."

"He's dangerous. You better call if there's a problem."

Her breath hitched. "He's not dangerous. He's just...he needs help." Her eyes shimmered with unshed tears. "Why do you pretend to care?"

Pretend? She had no clue. Nothing he did was fake. Half the time it took extreme strength to control himself. Like now. He was finding it very difficult not to grab the back of her head and kiss her senseless.

"It's my job." *Smooth answer, idiot.* Well, he wasn't looking for a relationship, so he couldn't say anything else.

"Have a nice day, Officer Crowl."

She effectively dismissed him. He deserved that. Why had he started the entire conversation about her brother anyway? He leaned back as he pulled a five-dollar bill from his wallet. Oh, yeah, he did it because he needed to keep his distance. Making her hate him would help accomplish that goal.

He threw the five down and grabbed his coffee. Any trace of happiness she had disappeared. His eyes glided to the necklace around her neck. What would it hurt?

"Can you make my mother a necklace for Christmas? I think she'd like one."

Theresa's hand shot to the one around her neck, fingering the beads. Her face bloomed a light shade of red.

"I'm pretty...my orders lately...I'm sorry. I don't think I'll have time to complete it before Christmas."

Whack! It's as if she had slapped him. He had a hard time believing she couldn't get it done in time. There were still two weeks left before Christmas. She just didn't want to make him one. He didn't blame her one bit. He acted like a jerk almost all the time with her.

"No problem."

He walked away before he said something he'd regret. Or worse, did something he'd regret. Like pulling her across the counter and kissing her. The sound of the bell ringing as he pushed open the door had him glancing up at the mistletoe. Dumb thing. He never wanted to see another mistletoe in his life.

Long, quick strides to his vehicle made him feel like he was running. Well, wasn't he? He was good at running away from his problems. The best at it. He'd been doing it like an ace since Cynthia died. Shit. Maybe even before she died.

He stopped at his car, yanked his keys out of his pocket, and set his coffee on the hood. Before he could click the unlock button, a voice spoke. Glancing up, he didn't even pretend to hide his annoyance. Of course, that didn't deter Marybeth, the worse nuisance in town. Perhaps on the planet.

"Hello, Aiden. How are you?"

"Busy." He clicked the unlock button and moved forward

to get her to move back. He wanted to jump inside and drive far away. Just keep driving until he felt free and whole and like a normal human being for once. He didn't think that would ever happen again.

Except Marybeth didn't move and he stood way too close to her. He knew she'd had a real thing for Chief Duncan for the longest time, but she always had a perverse way of flirting with any man. Him included. Hating to be so in her face, he took a step back. She had the audacity to smirk and chuckle.

"Did you forget, silly?"

"About?"

She clucked her tongue, then rubbed a hand down his arm. "Oh, you did. Are you okay? I know it's hard with Cynthia gone, especially around the holidays, but it'll be okay."

He shook off her hand that insisted on resting on his. "I'm fine."

"Well, you weren't at the meeting yesterday."

"What meeting?"

She had the nerve to look peeved that he forgot whatever it was she thought he was supposed to remember. He honestly had no clue what she was talking about.

"The committee meeting that puts on the annual Christmas party. It's in a week and, while we have most things done, you said you'd help on the decorating crew."

"When did I ever say that?" He knew for damn sure he would never do something like that. Maybe when Cynthia was around, he would've been suckered into helping, her insisting it would be good for him. He'd cave because if he didn't do it, well, things could get real ugly real fast when he declined to do something for her.

"Last year. Remember? You made an off-hand comment

at the party about how some of the lights hung crooked and you could've done a better job. I asked if you'd help next year to put up the decorations and you said yes."

He sighed. Marybeth sure knew how to twist words to her liking. Just one of the many things he couldn't stand about her. He never liked her when Cynthia was alive and they were inseparable, and he sure didn't like her now. In fact, he had no reason anymore to be nice to her since Cynthia was gone. Except his mother would have his hide if he was rude. She raised him to be a gentleman, not an asshole. Of course, he kept acting like one with Theresa.

"I never said that."

"Yes, you did."

He couldn't recall the conversation word for word, but he knew he'd never volunteer to help hang decorations. He did remember how one string of lights hung sort of low, yet the way they were situated made it look like it was done intentionally. He was positive that's how he'd phrased it. And she never asked him to help this year. He hadn't even wanted to go to the party, but Bentley, his best friend, forced him to get out of the house. No one would be forcing him to go to the party this year.

"Well, it's too late now. I missed the meeting."

"No, it's not. I took notes. We can meet later to discuss them." Her eyes sparkled with mischief. "After your shift. At your house."

He pinched the bridge of his nose, feeling more tired than annoyed by Marybeth's clear way of trying to insert herself into his life. And why? Because Chief Duncan was now off the market? What made her think he'd ever want a relationship with her? Because it would be a cold day in hell before that happened.

"Officer Crowl, I'm sorry for..." Theresa's words died as

he turned his body slightly and she saw Marybeth standing in front of him. "Oh, you're busy. I didn't see you there, Marybeth."

"Theresa." Marybeth smiled, yet Aiden could see the disdain in her eyes.

"Never mind. I'll leave you two alone." Theresa turned to leave.

His hand shot out, grabbing hers before she could step out of his reach. Although the cold snaked around him, his hands freezing from the low temps outside, the warmth from her hand heated him up. All over. Inside and out. He almost dropped her hand from the electricity coursing through him—almost, but he couldn't. The ache of desire was too strong. Instead, he pulled her a few steps closer, tempted to drop her hand and wrap his arm around her waist so she could be as close to him as possible.

The feelings she invoked were so unwelcome. Regardless, he didn't drop his hand from hers.

"Marybeth was just reminding me I volunteered to help hang decorations for the annual Christmas party. I forgot about it." Lies. He never volunteered in the first place. But an idea formed the second he grabbed her hand, and he couldn't seem to toss it aside.

"Okay." Theresa glanced at their hands, then back to his face just as quickly. "I'll let you guys talk about that."

"You should be there, too."

"I should?"

"She should?"

The surprise in both of their voices didn't surprise him. What surprised him was that he actually agreed to volunteer *and* that he wanted Theresa there.

"You have a knack for decorating. You said you enjoyed decorating. You can help me."

Theresa's eyes narrowed. Would she call him out on his bullshit? The slight glare in her eyes said she might, because she never told him she enjoyed decorating. Although, he liked how she decorated her tree, so that wasn't a lie. She had a knack for it.

She nodded once. "Sure, I don't mind helping."

He glanced back at Marybeth and almost produced a smile. His heart suddenly felt lighter. As if he'd been waiting for a moment like this. To lift his spirits for once.

"Why don't you just give me those notes you took and Theresa and I will take a look at them?"

Marybeth pursed her lips. Then a silky smile appeared. "I'll drop them off later. The party is next Saturday. Mrs. Contreas wants everything up on Friday. Do not be late or forget."

"We'll be there." He squeezed Theresa's hand, but she didn't say anything.

Marybeth gave him a saucy smile, with no glance at Theresa, and walked away.

Holding Theresa's hand was starting to make him itch with desire. So much so, he wanted to pull her roughly into his arms and kiss her. He was just about to let his control snap and do just that when she yanked her hand free and took a step back.

"What was that?"

HER HAND still tingled from his touch. The confusion swirled around them with the brisk cold wind.

"I figured you'd enjoy it."

Her eyes bulged out. He didn't know her at all. No clue whatsoever about her likes and dislikes. Because she did *not* want to help decorate for the annual Christmas party. Why would she? She'd never been invited to it in her life. Growing up in the dismal part of town ensured that never happened.

"Why would you think that? I've never been to the Christmas party before."

He frowned, his eyes narrowing, obviously trying to remember if she'd ever been to one. Which she hadn't.

"Haven't you ever wanted to go?"

"No."

She opened her mouth to elaborate, but decided against it. He didn't need to know she always felt inadequate around Marybeth, Cynthia, and all the other girls that always made her life miserable in high school. They were always the bell of the ball, so to speak. Why would she want to surround herself with people like that? And around Christmas, a holiday she loved. All it would do was make her hate the holiday.

"You lied. You know I never said I enjoyed decorating."

He shrugged. "Yeah, but you have a knack for it. I never even volunteered to help. I don't know what scheme Marybeth's playing."

A lame laugh filtered out. "Tell me you're not really that dumb."

The second those words came out, she felt ashamed of herself. What right did she have to speak to him like that? She twisted around to return to the café as fast as she could.

A hand shot out and grabbed hers, then spun her around. "You can't just walk away from me."

"Well, I just did. You'll be late for work."

He took a step closer. "Are you going to help me decorate or not?"

Yanking her hand out of his as politely as possible—

because she couldn't take how wonderful it felt for him to hold her hand—she nodded once. "I said I would."

"Don't look so happy about it."

"Why do you even want my help? If you're trying to make Marybeth jealous, I'd be the last person to accomplish that goal with. I'm nothing compared to her."

His face turned hard, his lips curling into the most disgusted look she'd ever seen from him. Exactly what she thought. He agreed. Why else would he look so disgusted?

"You honestly believe that?"

With a helpless shrug, she averted her eyes. "It's not like her or Cynth—" Her eyes darted to his. The look of disgust was gone, replaced with stoic indifference. "Just let me know when and I'll be there to help."

She turned around before more idiotic words came out of her mouth and hurried back to the café. The cold weather was starting to freeze her to the bone. While she could handle the cold, she had darted out of the café without grabbing her jacket before he could drive away. Or did she feel frozen to the bone from the terrible interaction with Officer Crowl? Why did she always act like an idiot around him?

Her hand grasped the cold handle of the diner door and pulled it open. Before she could step into the warmth, a hand touched her shoulder. She knew without looking who it would be. She turned slightly, almost resting against the open door. His hand fell to his side.

"You followed me outside for a reason. Why is that?"

She had almost forgotten why. Now she wished she never had the crazy impulse. But her conscience wouldn't let it go.

"I'm sorry."

Confusion muddled his features. "For what?"

"For being so rude earlier."

He rubbed his jaw, then looked away. "Forget about Marybeth. Forget about everything that just happened."

She took a step toward the warmth of the diner, wanting to be finished with the conversation already. "Not about that. Although I am sorry if I said anything to offend you."

His eyes locked with hers. "You didn't. But I'm confused as hell. Why are you sorry?"

She let out a huge breath. "For saying I couldn't make your mother a necklace. I can make one."

"I don't want to put more on your plate, Theresa. You already have some orders to take care of, not to mention working at the diner. Now you're helping with the decorations..." A terrified panic entered his eyes. "You are going to help me, right?"

"I said I would."

His lips pressed into a thin line, yet nothing came out.

"What kind of necklace would you like?"

He sighed, then relaxed his features. "Her favorite color is yellow. I'm sure whatever you come up with will be beautiful." He took a step closer to her. "I have no doubt about that."

"Well, then. That's settled. Have a good day."

He leaned in, a breath away. "Are things really settled between us?"

"Of course. You should get to work."

"I should." His soft lips landed on hers, exerting a small amount of pressure, then just as quickly, he backed away.

He took three steps toward his vehicle before she yelled, "What was that?"

Twisting to look at her, he looked at her deadpan, but with a tiny twinkle in his eyes. "Mistletoe." He continued to walk away.

She turned and stepped inside, letting the door close behind her. Looking up, she eyed the mistletoe hanging. Odd. He was blaming the mistletoe again. But this time they hadn't been standing directly underneath it. They were outside and the mistletoe hung inside. Did it still count if you weren't standing directly underneath it?

She didn't understand him at all. What was going on? What was he doing to her?

She touched her lips with her fingers.

Did it matter what he was doing? He kissed her on the lips.

She dropped her fingers and shook her head at the silly notions running through her mind. It didn't mean anything. He would never like her like that. Never in a million years.

5

AIDEN PULLED behind the fire truck, his lights flashing but the sirens off. As he stepped out of his vehicle, the lights lit up the dark night sky, yet nothing could light up the ugliness inside him. Nothing but—

There he was thinking things he shouldn't again. Since he walked away from the diner, from Theresa, that's all he'd been doing. Thinking. His thoughts just had a mind of their own, and he hated it. With a passion.

He walked between his car and the fire truck into the ditch and saw a car positioned at an angle. The front of the car looked damaged. It'd take a miracle from a seasoned mechanic to fix it. No dents appeared on the bumper, a decent indication the person driving lost control on their own, not hit from behind.

He took a few steps down into the ditch and noticed an ambulance parked in front of the fire truck. A middle-aged man sat inside the ambulance while Chasity, the paramedic, held some white gauze to his head. Instead of heading for the ambulance, Aiden made the rest of his way down the ditch to the vehicle where his best friend, and one of the firefighters, Bentley, stood by the busted up vehicle.

"What happened?" He tried not to cringe from the cold, wet snow seeping into his shoes.

"Pretty sure he's drunk as a skunk. Swerved right off the road and into the ditch. Nasty cut on the forehead, otherwise, unharmed." Bentley tossed his head toward the ambulance. "Asshole's lucky he didn't hit anyone else. He stumbled the entire way to the ambulance."

"DUI. My favorite." He walked around to the front where Bentley stood. "What are you doing here?"

"We were driving by. We were called to the Daughtry Farm because their five-year-old decided it would be cool to climb a tree after being dared by his seven-year-old brother, but then couldn't get down. Of course, they didn't have a ladder tall enough." He bent down and pointed. "Looks like scrapes of white paint. I'm thinking knucklehead up there might've hit something before he crashed his car. What do you think?"

"I think I'm going to have a long night ahead of me." He wasn't mad or annoyed about it either. Better to be busy than have time to himself to think.

Bentley slapped a hand to his shoulder and squeezed. "You live for this shit. But you look out of it. More so than usual. You okay, man?"

"I'm good."

A slow grin emerged on Bentley's face. "You sure? I heard some rumors."

He rolled his eyes, not even willing to hide his annoyance. What lies was Marybeth spinning? "Like what?"

"Oh, I don't know." A low chuckle left his mouth. "Something about you and Theresa."

Okay. That was unexpected.

"And where did you hear these rumors? What rumors exactly?"

"Well, Daphne said—"

"Stop." He held his hand up to halt any more asinine comments. "Daphne loves to spread gossip. She never stops talking. Whatever she said is not true." He tilted his head, curling his lips just a smidge. "Haven't you gotten over your little crush on her? Why were you talking to her? She's been dating her boyfriend for the past two years and loves him to death."

"The guy is an idiot. Who dates a beautiful, smart, gorgeous woman like her for that long and doesn't put a ring on her finger? An idiot, that's who."

He tried not to wince at those words. Bentley could call him an idiot then. He waited years to ask Cynthia to marry him. Actually, he didn't even ask her. It was more like, "Let's get married next fall. I have the perfect ring picked out that I just adore." She didn't hesitate as she said it, or think anything strange about him not saying a peep. He was a little too stunned. Even more surprised when his mom called him to congratulate him. Cynthia just bulldozed over him and told his mom before he could.

Although Bentley knew that. He couldn't help but tell someone how she sort of railroaded him into marriage. The only part he didn't tell Bentley was how much he didn't want to marry her but went along with it because that's just what he did. He always listened to her without fail.

"Dude, did you hear me?" Bentley grinned deviously. "You have a thing for Theresa or what? Since when do you help the decorating committee for the Christmas party..."

Because Cynthia's not here. Bentley's unspoken words. He didn't have to say it. He just knew what he meant.

"Since Marybeth suckered me into it and..." Shit. How

could he explain dragging Theresa into it without making it look like he liked her? He couldn't. Because, damn it, he did like her. He just didn't want to.

Bentley's smile died as he landed another hand to his shoulder and squeezed. This time in sympathy. "Dude. It's been over a year. It's okay to meet someone new and move on. Cynthia—"

"I should go talk to the drunk guy and slap some handcuffs on him. The fire department is free to leave. I've got it now."

Bentley pierced him with a hard stare, then nodded, knowing damn well when Aiden didn't want to talk, nothing was going to change his mind. Not even his best friend. Bentley didn't even know the truth about Cynthia's death. Nobody did. He'd kept that secret hidden inside so long, it was engraved on his heart. He'd never bare it to another soul. He deserved the misery for what he had done to her.

"Wanna get a beer on your day off?"

"Yeah, sure. I'll talk to you later." Aiden walked away before Bentley could pelt him with more words he didn't want to hear. He had a long night ahead of him. He had to book a drunk idiot and investigate whether he hit anything else. Drinking and driving was one of his worst pet peeves. People with no care or concern for anyone else but themselves. The guy had what was coming to him. If he found out he hit something else, he planned to throw every little charge he could at the guy.

Yeah, it was going to be a very long night. He almost smiled at the thought. Because then his mind wouldn't wander to things he shouldn't think about.

Like Theresa's beautiful face and the look of shock after he kissed her on the lips. Oh, how he wanted to dip his tongue in and show her what a kiss between them would truly feel like. He settled for a quick peck that left him aching for more. So much more.

What was she doing right now? Sleeping, perhaps. Making necklaces. Watching TV by herself...or with someone? Did she have someone in her life that he didn't know about?

Not his concern. Theresa wasn't anything more than a friend. That's it. He'd do well to remember that. If there was a guy in her life, he'd know. Because Daphne would've never started to spread rumors about them if Theresa had a boyfriend. Why had she done that to begin with? She obviously had nothing better to do.

He stopped at the back of the ambulance, a fierce scowl on his face. Time for work mode. Although, right before he started to question the drunk guy, he realized something that made him shiver with unease. He'd been thinking too much the last few days. Nothing new there. Except the person he had been thinking about.

His thoughts always turned to Cynthia and the horrible way he had treated her. The past few days, most of his thoughts had centered around Theresa.

Not good. At all.

If he could pull out a picture of Cynthia to remind himself of why it'd be bad to think about Theresa even a little bit, he would. Except he destroyed or gave away all the photos he had of her. He couldn't stand the reminder of his failures. Of what he had done.

Settling for conjuring an image of her would have to suffice. He had to remove thoughts of Theresa out of his mind. In any possible way.

Because nothing good would come from thinking about her. Or liking her.

He'd just end up killing her like he had Cynthia.

THERESA GOT HOME on time with no problems with her brother, although he wasn't returning her phone calls, so she kind of considered that a problem. She made supper, worked on the orders that were starting to pile up, and tried not to think about Officer Crowl...Aiden. No. Officer Crowl. She needed to keep her distance. Especially when every time she saw him lately, his actions confused her.

Why did he keep kissing her every time they were near some mistletoe?

By eleven o'clock, her fingers were tingling with soreness from stringing bead after bead after bead. But the important thing was she finished Officer Crowl's necklace for his mother. Yeah, she had plenty of orders ahead of his, but the sooner she finished, the better everything would be. She was still trying to come up with a good excuse to get out of helping him decorate for the Christmas party. Although, any excuse that crossed her mind was so pathetic she knew he'd see right through the lie. She figured she just had to help him and move on.

Just move on. She could do that.

She went to bed, dreaming delicious things of a certain man she shouldn't, and woke up feeling more tired than when she went to bed.

After a quick cup of coffee, a small berating for forgetting—again—to unplug her Christmas tree, which she immediately rectified when she saw it lit up, she called her brother. Still no answer. Unless he was drinking, he never ignored her. She wouldn't put it past him to be drunk this early in the morning. He could party into the early morning hours. To some people, nine o'clock wasn't that early. To her brother, it was the butt crack of dawn.

Regardless, she worried about him. She hadn't spoken to him since she bailed him out, and she had a dreadful suspicion he never got the help he insisted he would get. Her fault, really. She trusted him to do the right thing. Every. Single. Time.

Every time, he disappointed her. She should know better by now. So much for Officer Crowl's tough love approach. Even spending the night in jail had done nothing to change his ways. She wasn't surprised.

Still. She had to make sure he was okay.

Grabbing her winter coat and scarf and wrapping it tightly around her neck, she headed the few blocks to her brother's house. Or more like the place he crashed at the most. He didn't have a permanent address. While she felt bad for not letting him live with her, she knew it'd be the worst mistake she'd ever make. Which was why she never offered. He'd steal from her and make her life more miserable than it already was when she had to deal with his drunken ass.

She didn't like his friend Dusty, who always had too grabby of hands. She never said anything to him other than "Keep your hands to yourself." She even had to slap his hand away a few times when he had tried to grab her ass. She could tell her brother. While he could be downright mean to her when he was drinking, he was still her big brother. He'd hurt anyone who hurt her. She didn't want to see him get into trouble for beating Dusty to pieces. Because he totally would.

She took a fortifying breath, hoping against all hope Dusty wasn't home, and knocked on the door. The temperature was in the low thirties. She wanted to check on her brother, then hightail it home. She was freezing. Her hands were numb to the bone even though she had on the warmest gloves she owned. Even sticking them in her jacket pockets did little to shield the cold from sweeping in.

A sigh of relief left her mouth when her brother opened the door. Then she frowned when a hint of alcohol drifted her way.

"You're drunk. Already?"

"What do you want, Tessy?"

Well, that was a good sign. He only called her by her childhood nickname when he was sober, or mostly sober. Maybe the smell was from last night's bender. Which was still bad. He didn't get the help he said he would.

"Did you go to an AA meeting? Did you go anywhere like you said you would? A treatment center? Anything?"

James closed his eyes and groaned. "You seriously walked all the way here to ask me that dumb question?" He opened his eyes with a mean glare. "Go home, Tessy. I'm sorry for bothering you the other night. It won't happen again. I don't have a problem."

She could've laughed, but that would've only made him angry. "I worry about you—"

"Go home." He started to close the door on her.

She slapped her hand to the door before he could completely shut it. "Wait!"

"What? I'm not about to listen to your whining. It's too damn early for this shit."

She let her hand fall away from the door and started to twist her hands together. So maybe her only reason for coming wasn't just to see how he was doing. "Can I...uh... borrow your car?" His eyes narrowed. "Just for, like, an hour or two. Not too long."

"For what?"

Seriously? He constantly badgered her for money, banging on her door in the middle of the night, breaking into her home to steal from her, and he had the audacity to question her about why she wanted to use his car. She rarely asked him for anything. Telling him the truth would be stressful. He probably wouldn't take it well. He hated Officer Crowl, a clear indication by the fact he hit him. Sure, he was drunk, but he never had a pleasant thing to say about him even when he was sober.

She couldn't ask Bonzo to borrow his truck because he'd ask questions, too. Damn it. She just didn't want to answer anyone's questions.

"Does it matter? I don't ask you for a lot of things. Forget about paying me back the bail money. Just let me borrow your car this morning." That was laughable. He even chuckled at her words. They both knew he wouldn't be paying her back regardless. He never had enough money.

"Whatever. Hold on a sec." He shut the door.

She stood there waiting patiently. For a long time it seemed. She was starting to get nervous that he decided to ignore her request when the door swung open again. He held out the car keys, then snatched them closer to his chest when she reached for them.

"Tell me what you need the car for."

"Sign up for an AA meeting or treatment facility and I will."

"Tessy, why do you care so much? So I drink a little. It's nothing."

Her shoulders drooped as a wave of sadness washed over her. Did he really not see the similarities between him and their dad? Did he not see he was turning out just like the drunken bastard he swore he'd never turn into when he was a teenager?

"You grabbed me the other night. By the wrist. Do you even remember doing that? It almost hurt. Your grip was strong." He stepped back as if she slapped him. "You're my brother and I'll always care about you, even when you act like an ass."

"I'd never..." He let out a heavy breath. "I'd never hurt you, Tessy. I'm sorry, okay?"

She held out her hand. "I forgive you."

He tossed the keys to her, then slammed the door shut. It didn't faze her. He never liked to hear how much he hurt her, but she wasn't going to lie to him. He needed to realize what his actions were doing. Yet, he never did. He just kept drinking more and more.

Maybe getting arrested and spending a night in jail was a good thing. Maybe the judge would see the problem he had. Maybe the judge would order treatment. Maybe Officer Crowl had been right all along.

Well, she'd probably never admit that to him. She wasn't about to admit anything. Especially how she felt about him, or how much he kept confusing her with his erratic behavior. One minute cold towards her, and the next minute so hot he's kissing her on the lips.

She started her brother's car and put it into drive, wondering if she was making the biggest mistake of her life. Knocking on Officer Crowl's door seemed like a dumb decision. There was no reason she couldn't wait until Monday afternoon when she worked again to give him the necklace.

Okay, she had a reason. She just wanted to see him. To kiss him. To find out the real reason why he wanted her to help decorate.

Like the chicken she was, she knew none of that would come out of her mouth.

She drove to his home, about a twenty-minute drive, considering he lived on the nicer side of town, but also on the outskirts. He had a few neighbors, although they were all spaced out fairly decently. They weren't in shouting distance of each other. She didn't think anyone would have a need to shout, especially him. He didn't display much emotion anymore. Sadness overwhelmed her at the thought.

The driveway was long, trees covering the view of his home. The woods surrounding the property lifted her spirits a little after the tense encounter with her brother. Something beautiful always managed to do that, and the latest dusting of snow covered the ground with such magical intent. Just a little more snow and it'd be perfect to build a snowman. She hadn't created one of those since her child-hood. An old scarf to wrap around his thick neck. A ratty old knit hat to place atop his snowy head. Some rocks they'd find mingled in the plowed snow for eyes and a nose. A few sticks to create a wicked looking mouth and arms that curved out with merriment. She and her brother always had fun building a snowman.

She wondered briefly as she pulled to a stop by the front porch how long it took him to shovel his driveway. He prob-ably had to use a snow blower. An hour? When she stepped out, she couldn't stop her curiosity and glanced around the property, since this was her first time visiting him. A funny looking piece of machinery caught her eye near the side of the house. Was that a Bobcat? Was that how he shoveled his driveway? He plowed it?

There were a few mounds of snow on each side of the driveway, making her assume that's what he did. The latest snowfall last week hadn't been too much, but the week before that, they had gotten eleven inches. The first snowfall of the season and it had been a doozy. On days like that, Bonzo never let her walk. He was at her door, honking the horn to signal he was ready to pick her up for work. The days since then hadn't been warm enough to melt much of the snow.

She didn't see his car anywhere, although she figured he probably parked it inside the garage. Slow, even steps across his porch felt like the walk of doom. Why was she here? Would he slam the door in her face? Would he finally kiss her breathless?

Ha! Yeah, right. Like he wanted to do that. Those other kisses didn't mean anything. Just a simple peck under the mistletoe. Because that's what a person did when you stood under one.

She raised her hand to knock, then froze. He worked the night shift. He probably didn't get home until midnight or later. She honestly didn't know when his shift ended. Maybe he was still sleeping. Although, it was almost ten o'clock. Maybe he was awake.

But what if he wasn't? He probably wouldn't appreciate her waking him up. What a terrible idea. Hadn't she told herself this was a mistake? Yes, she had. She should leave.

The door swung open.

"Theresa?"

He looked upset. Brows burrowed low, lips thinned into a tight line. And the way he said her name, so full of wrath.

Oh, boy. He wasn't just upset at her. He was downright pissed.

6

AIDEN COULDN'T BELIEVE his eyes. It's as if his thoughts had conjured the one thing he couldn't stop thinking about. Why was she here?

He heard someone pull into his driveway as he sat at the dining room table having a cup of coffee. When he heard no knock or ringing of the doorbell, he figured he should check it out. He had been tempted to grab his firearm from his bedroom, but nixed the idea. Not much bad happened in their small town of Mulberry.

"What are you doing here?"

That came out sounding harsher than he intended. But he was upset. Just so damn pissed he dreamt about her all night, picturing her gorgeous body next to his. Then this morning, his mind still skipped around in circles wondering what she was doing at that very moment. Still sleeping? Having a cup of coffee like him? Working on her necklaces?

It all pissed him off.

"I'm so sorry to bother you. This was a mistake."

She turned around and scampered down the stairs so

fast that her feet slipped on the frosty ground and she landed hard, knocking her head against the ground.

"Theresa!"

He scrambled out of the house so quickly he didn't even register he was walking on the cold snow with bare feet. She moaned as he knelt by her side.

"Are you okay?" When she moaned again as she felt the back of her head, he didn't care whether she could walk on her own. He scooped her up with ease and headed for the house as quickly and safely as he could.

He closed the door with a kick of his foot and walked to the living room where he gently laid her down. And damn if he didn't want to continue holding her instead.

"Let me see. I sure hope you didn't crack your head open. You fell hard." He knelt by her side and tenderly lifted her head, feeling with his hands and searching carefully with his eyes for any sign of blood. He saw nothing of concern, although he could feel a small bump on the back of her head. "How's your butt feeling? Head looks okay besides a tiny bump."

"Like I fell on it hard." She chuckled, yet her eyes didn't shine with laughter as they normally did when she laughed. "I'm okay. I should go."

"Stay." He stood up. "Just rest for a moment. I'll go get you something warm to drink. Coffee?"

She nodded, but said nothing.

He quickly walked out of the room but took his time pouring her a cup of coffee. Why had she come? Had she felt the intense attraction for him that he felt for her? He couldn't give her anything. Nothing that would keep her in his life for the long term. Just the idea of long term had his body convulsing with tremors. He could never do forever, even as badly as he wanted it with somebody.

But it had been so long since he'd slept with anyone. Too long. Even before Cynthia died, he had a dry spell for a few months because connecting with her had been difficult to do. His entire body ached. Badly. He needed to release all of the tension.

Theresa wasn't that kind of girl. He'd never use her as a fun toy, then kick her to the curb. She deserved more than that. She didn't need a man in her life who would let her down, or worse, hurt her beyond repair.

When he walked back into the living room with her coffee, he knew he'd have a helluva time keeping his hands to himself. It wasn't right to want her the way he did, and he could feel himself slowly losing the control he tried so hard to keep a hold of.

"Here." He sat on the edge of the couch near her legs and held out the mug.

She scooted her butt a little to sit up better and took the mug. He was so thankful not one finger touched his. Just the smallest contact might've sent him into a frenzy. One little touch and he'd have her naked in under five seconds flat. Although he was sitting near her legs, not one part of him was touching her.

"Thank you."

"How's everything feeling? You fell hard. Do you need to go to the hospital?"

She shook her head, then winced from the movement. "I'm fine."

"That didn't look fine."

"Just a small headache. It's nothing to worry about. I'm sorry for barging in on you."

He ached to touch her. To reach out his hand and stroke her cheek, her arm, anything. "Why are you here? How do you even know where I live?"

She chuckled, this time with the laughter in her eyes. It made his heart soar from the beauty of it. "Small town. I think everyone knew when you put an offer in last year. Heck, before you even thought of putting an offer in."

He couldn't help it. He chuckled, his lips almost curling into a smile. "So true. A bunch of gossipers. Daphne's the worst, although she doesn't mean it maliciously." Then his lips turned down into a low frown. "Please tell me you didn't walk here."

"Didn't you see the car parked outside?"

He wanted to smack himself in the face. No, he didn't see it. All he saw was how beautiful she looked standing on his porch. How much he ached to pull her into his arms. How pissed he was for feeling that way. Then all he saw was fear and rage that she could've hurt herself. And why? Because of him.

All he ever did was hurt people.

His frown turned fierce. "Whose car?"

She averted her eyes. "My brother's."

He jerked to his feet, clearly upset. Couldn't she see how dangerous her brother was to be around? "If you feel better, you should go." He didn't even care why she came or that she borrowed her brother's car. At least she didn't walk all the way here.

She slowly turned and set her feet on the floor, then leaned forward to put her coffee down on the small table in front of the couch. Standing up, she avoided his eyes. "I'm sorry if I upset you somehow." Without a word, he let her walk toward the front door.

Wait. No, damn it. He wanted to know why she came here.

He followed her, amazed at how fast she made it to the front door. She was obviously eager to leave. Before she could open the door all the way, he slammed it shut. She stumbled as she turned around in surprise, and her back fell lightly against the door. He moved closer, effectively boxing her in.

A sweet scent of roses drifted his way, reeling him in even closer.

"Why did you come?"

"I..." Her eyes glossed to his lips that were precariously close to hers. "I finished your mother's necklace. I just wanted to drop it off."

That's not the reason he expected. It pissed him off. The anger stirring in his veins before she arrived skyrocketed. Perhaps she didn't feel the connection he felt.

He was about to find out. Because he couldn't hold it in any longer. He needed to feel her lips against his.

His lips grazed hers. Tentatively at first, then more insistent. A low moan echoed throughout the hallway, giving him the confirmation that she wanted more just like him. His tongue swooped in as her arms circled around his neck.

Yes. She felt wonderful in his arms. So soft. So sweet. So his for the taking.

He pressed closer to her, the kiss turning hotter than he intended. Because he couldn't control himself. Not when he had dreamt about Theresa the last few nights. His dreams didn't compare to the real thing. Theresa felt so right in his arms.

No!

He abruptly broke the kiss and backed away.

He shouldn't be kissing her. He shouldn't be enjoying it. None of this was right. It couldn't be.

"Why did you just kiss me?" Her eyes narrowed instantly. "And don't give me that mistletoe crap. There's no mistletoe here." Although she must've doubted her words because she glanced up to make sure there was no mistletoe hanging.

For once, he had no good excuse for why he kissed her. How could he explain he wouldn't be good for her? That he'd end up hurting her?

"You should leave."

The hurt in her eyes was swift and painful to look at.

"I don't understand you, Officer Crowl." She sighed, then turned around and pulled the door open. It closed with a quiet click.

Why did she always call him that? Thinking back, he couldn't remember one time where she had called him Aiden. He wanted to hear his name on her lips. Just once.

No. What he wanted was to forget about her.

Locking the door, to add an extra measure of security to his impulses, he almost ran to his bedroom so he wouldn't be tempted to watch her leave. Hell, the temptation to rush out there and stop her ran unbridled through his veins.

What was wrong with him?

A beautiful, easy-going, wonderful woman seemed to like him just as much as he liked her, and he pushed her away by acting like a world-class jerk.

Sitting on the edge of his bed, his hands in his lap, the loneliness engulfing him, he realized Theresa never gave him the necklace.

A very good reason to seek her out was right before his eyes.

Sinking back into the bed, his eyes glossed over in madness as he stared at the ceiling.

Would it hurt to let someone in for once? It already hurt keeping people out. Could it really hurt much worse?

It didn't matter. Theresa deserved better than him.

Someone who didn't kill the person they loved, like him.

Of course, the day Cynthia died, he hadn't loved her anymore.

That just made what happened a hundred times worse.

***

THERESA WIPED her hands on her jeans before pulling open the door to Lynn's bakery. Only thirty degrees outside today and her hands were sweating.

Who was she kidding? Her entire body was still on fire since the latest kiss with Officer Crowl. He had left her so flustered, she didn't even put her gloves back on before she left his house. She left them in her pocket, even when she got into her car and drove away.

He had moments of grumpiness, of being so indifferent it bordered on rude. But today...he broke her heart. One second he's kissing her as if he'd drown if he let her go, and in the next second, he's telling her to get the hell out. Well, at least he said it nicely, but she heard the tone in his voice. You should leave translated into *get the hell out.*

She read him loud and clear. From now on, she wouldn't be as nice. He wanted to act that way with her without an explanation for his actions, fine. She tended to let people run all over her. Her mother. Her brother. Bonzo, on occasion, but he did it because he worried about her. She was done letting Officer Crowl do it.

And no more kissing.

"Theresa, what a surprise." Lynn's brows puckered as she boxed up a batch of cookies from the front display case for Mrs. Miner. "Are you okay?"

Plastering on a smile, she nodded. "I was driving by and saw how busy you are. Thought I'd offer my help. You shouldn't make such delicious baked goods, especially around Christmas time."

Lynn laughed with her and tossed her head toward the swinging door that led to the kitchen of the bakery. "There's an extra apron hanging on the pegs to the left. I would love some help."

The smile in her eyes didn't mask the concern. Lynn wanted to know what was going on, and eventually Theresa might tell her. But right now, she just wanted to work this frustration out. Going home to work on her jewelry, while it would be good to get ahead of the orders she had, didn't sound appealing. She didn't want to be alone.

Pushing open the door, she smiled at Gabby, who was standing at a counter bagging loafs of cinnamon swirl bread. Oh, man, Lynn made the best cinnamon swirl bread. Her mouth started to water at the sight of the deliciousness staring her in the face and the wondrous scents drifting to her nose.

"Hi, Theresa."

She grabbed an apron hanging not far from her. "Hi, Gabby. I thought I'd help out some. Excited for Christmas?"

Her eyes beamed wide with happiness. "Oh, yes. All of my kids are coming home for Christmas. Gregory insists that they all come over to his house, and I'm sure I'll give in. I just don't want to intrude on Elliot and Lynn."

"I'm sure they don't mind. And I imagine Gregory is already going nuts with presents."

Gabby laughed with delight. "You know it."

The last time she experienced a Christmas filled with presents galore and family filling the house, almost over-crowding the place, was when she was younger, before her dad had really started to drink. His family and her mother's side used to visit all the time, especially around the holidays. The house boomed with laughter and joy, presents piled high under the tree, and all the food they cooked and baked left the counters with no room for anything else. She missed those days. The last few years she had a quiet dinner with her mom, and if she was lucky, her brother. Her dad didn't come around anymore. Heck, she didn't even know where he was. Maybe living in St. Cloud.

This year would be one of the loneliest Christmases by far. Her mother met someone a few months ago. His family was from Ireland, and she left last week for a month-long vacation with his family. Like the free-spirited woman she could be, she left without much of a goodbye, or an offer to join her for Christmas. She probably would've declined because her boyfriend was a little odd, and she didn't want to spend the holidays with people she didn't know. But an offer would've been nice.

Heck, maybe she would've said yes. Ireland sounded like a great place to visit.

Theresa tied the apron around her waist and internally debated whether she should help Gabby or go out by Lynn when the door swung open.

"Hi, Chief Duncan." Theresa smiled at him as she patted the front of her apron, suddenly nervous and very self-conscious. Which was silly. Just because Chief Duncan was Officer Crowl's boss didn't mean he knew she kissed him.

"Hey, Theresa." He smiled. "Lynn mentioned you just got here. I thought I'd lend a hand as well. Why don't you head out by Lynn and I'll tackle whatever Gabby needs me to do back here?" He threw a special smile to Gabby. "My dad's out front. He wants to go shopping for a few more gifts. He mentioned you might want to tag along with him and Laura."

Gabby chuckled as she started to untie her apron. "That silly man has no control. I better make sure he doesn't buy the entire store."

Chief Duncan laughed. "You know him. There's no stopping him sometimes."

Gabby patted his shoulder in a motherly gesture and then left.

An awkward silence drifted between them.

"Are you okay, Theresa?"

She nodded, afraid if she said anything, the wrong words would come out. Something crazy like "Why does Officer Crowl like me one moment, then hate me the next?" That would be the dumbest thing she could possibly say. She really wanted to know, though.

Before he could say anything else, she slipped out the doors to the front. Lynn put her to work immediately refilling the display cases and helping the customers as they steadily stopped in for the delicious baked goods Lynn created with a magic touch.

Two hours later, sweat trickled down her back and her armpits were wet with the energy she exerted running back and forth from counter to counter. But, thankfully, the rush was over.

Leaning against the counter, she swiped a lock of hair out of her eyes and blew out a breath. "Is it like this every day? Because, seriously, you should hire someone to help you."

"I've thought about it. I could probably afford to hire one person, and it would give me more time at home. I feel like I'm always working. When I'm not here, Elliot is. He's such a sweetheart. Even Gabby helps me out so much."

Theresa smiled at the joy on Lynn's face. Why couldn't

she have something like her? A beautiful relationship with a man who did the most wonderful things for her just because he wanted to. She couldn't imagine Officer Crowl showing up to her home to help her string beads. Ha! She couldn't even imagine him dropping by just for a visit.

"I appreciate the help." Lynn leaned against the counter as she pierced a friendly but hard glare at her. "Now tell me what's bugging you. You walked in here with the saddest look I've ever seen from you. Is everything okay?"

Untying her apron, she nodded. "I wanted to say thank you for sending so much work my way. I can't believe how many jewelry orders I have before Christmas. I'm just not used to all this work. I'm a little tired."

"And here you are, helping me out. I—"

"No! I wanted to help. Don't feel bad." Theresa set the apron on the counter near where Lynn was resting. The look on Lynn's face portrayed she didn't believe a word she said. "I love making jewelry." She shrugged, looking away. "I guess I just didn't want to go home to an empty house." She glanced back at Lynn. "I don't want to talk about it, if that's okay."

"Of course it's okay. I didn't mean to pry." Lynn stood straighter and grabbed a hug before she could protest. "I know what it's like to need a friend. I just want you to know I'll be here for you whenever you're ready to talk about it."

"Thanks, Lynn."

"Oh...uh...I'll just...yeah."

Lynn chuckled at Elliot's retreating back as he went through the swinging doors without another word, then she moved away from Theresa. "He's so adorable when he gets tongue-tied. Laura asked him the other day about boys acting a certain way and he blushed like a big red light bulb, stuttering over his words."

"You found a great guy." Theresa chuckled to ease the awkwardness floating between them. Unless she was the only one feeling it. "I should probably go home and get some of those orders done."

"Thanks again for your help."

Theresa smiled as she walked out. Time to drop off her brother's car and go home to an empty house. None of that sounded like fun.

But a nice bubble bath sounded like a great plan. And a glass of wine.

That's what she'd do. Screw making jewelry. She needed one night to herself just relaxing. To get her mind off a man who didn't merit an ounce of her thoughts. Not with the way he continued to treat her. Hot then cold. She couldn't take it anymore. She wouldn't.

If she saw Officer Crowl again, she would give him a piece of her mind.

Or completely ignore him. She wasn't sure she'd have enough bravery to call him out on his bullshit.

"HEY, mister. Go home. It shouldn't be too busy now."

Elliot wrapped Lynn into his warm embrace, kissing her soundly on the lips. It felt like years since he'd kissed her, when in reality it was only a few hours ago. Every time he kissed her, it was like coming home. It just felt right.

"Everything okay with Theresa? She seemed out of it or something."

Lynn chuckled as she rested her head against his chest. "Or something."

"Meaning?"

Looking up, she brushed her lips against his. "It's girl stuff. I don't want to bore you with it."

"In other words, you don't want to tell me."

"I do, but...I don't want to make it awkward for you or anything."

Elliot tensed as his brows rose. "Theresa has a thing..."

Her laughter echoed off the walls. "No, silly, that's not what I meant, although who wouldn't want a thing for you? Too bad you're all mine."

"Yes, you are." He suddenly picked her up, her legs wrapping around his waist, and started walking until her butt hit the edge of the counter. "You know what the smell of your delicious cookies does to me."

"Elliot, we're in my bakery. Don't be naughty." She giggled as he started to nibble on her neck in playful delight.

He kissed her tenderly on the lips, then cocked a brow. "So. Tell me what could be awkward."

Lynn debated with herself for about half a second, then decided she would never want him to keep secrets from her so she wouldn't start now either.

"I'm pretty sure Theresa likes Officer Crowl and...I could be wrong, but I think he likes her, too."

The smile on his face dipped. "Aiden...well...he hasn't been the same since his fiancé died. I like him, but I'm not sure he'd be a good fit for Theresa. She has enough problems with her brother. Not to mention, Aiden arrested him."

"She's the one who called the cops. Her brother hit him. That wasn't Aiden's fault."

"True." He rubbed his face, then pulled her tighter into his body. "Is there something brewing in that beautiful mind of yours?"

"Not really. I just want everybody to be happy, especially around Christmas time."

Elliot kissed the top of her head. "I know you do, sweetheart. Maybe Santa will do what he did for us."

"Maybe," she whispered.

7

THERESA WISHED ON A LUCKY STAR, even though she couldn't see any in the broad daylight, that her brother would answer the door. Not Dusty.

Figures she wouldn't get lucky twice in one day.

The door swung open to Dusty's ugly face, his eyes glassy and red. The strong smell of alcohol drifted her way. Although she had a feeling it was a permanent odor that never left.

"Is my brother here?"

Dusty slumped against the doorframe, a wily grin appearing. "Just you and me, babe."

Her hand tightened around the car keys that were fisted in her jacket pocket. She had the strange urge to stab him in the eye, especially when he spoke to her in such a slimy tone.

"Just let him know I stopped by."

James could come get his car from her house. Not only did she not want to be in the same vicinity as Dusty, she didn't trust him enough to hand over the car keys. She turned around to leave.

"Whoa! What's the hurry?" Dusty reached out so quickly to grab her arm that she jerked against his chest. He took that opportunity to snake an arm around her and press her closer. "You smell like a cupcake."

"Let me go." She shivered with disgust as his face dipped closer, his hot breath fanning across her neck.

"Stay for a drink, darling."

He never understood the word no. But he'd understand this very clearly.

Her hand swung out of her pocket, the car key between her fingers, and slammed it down into his thigh. He screamed in pain and shoved her away.

She had no time to steady herself and fell down hard, her cheek grazing the cold cement sidewalk.

"You bitch!" Dusty hobbled before snatching the keys in front of him that had fallen from her hands. "You're damn lucky this shit didn't go through my jeans."

Even though her face hurt like hell, as did her knees that also landed hard, she scrambled to her feet and backed away. "No, Dusty, you're lucky I went easy on you. Don't ever touch me again. I don't think my brother would like to hear about it."

He laughed. The sound sent tiny tremors down her spine. "That dumbass doesn't scare me."

She started to slowly back away. "Well, I can also tell Officer Crowl." She never would, too embarrassed to even think about his grimy hands on her, but the look in Dusty's eyes said that thought scared him.

The vile sneer on his face made her want to run, but she held her ground, refusing to show him any fear. "Go home, Theresa. Be very careful. You never know what might happen."

She didn't respond to that, because honestly, what could

she say? She knew a threat when she heard one. If she said anything to Officer Crowl, Dusty would do something to her. She had no doubt about that. Well, it was a good thing she never intended to tell him.

As calmly as she could make it appear, she turned around and walked away. She could only hope Dusty gave James the car keys back without an issue. Because she had no intention of ever returning to that house. Not even if James called her.

By the time she made it home, the cold had numbed her to the bone. Although part of that was from Dusty's filthy hands on her. The disgust filled her from head to toe. She locked her door, double-checking it was secure, then all but ran to her laundry room where she removed her clothes and tossed them into the washing machine. Pouring in some detergent, she started a load without adding any other clothes. She just didn't care. Removing the evidence of his touch was all that mattered.

Walking calmly, yet the nerves running rampant through her veins, she hopped into the shower, turning the water as hot as it could go. For a few minutes, she just let the spray cleanse her. The warmth soothed her weary bones, soaking deep inside until the water started to scald her. Maybe it was a little too hot.

She found a better temperature and lathered herself up, washing every spot on her body. By the time she finished, she was as red as a tomato. Wrapping her big, fluffy white robe around her body, she tied the knot and cleared the mirror of steam with her hand.

"Damn." Leaning closer, she tenderly rubbed a finger down the small, ugly bruise that had started to form on her cheek. The pain wasn't intense when she pressed lightly on it, but it ached. She hit the ground hard for the second time, but she didn't think she cracked any bones. She figured she would've felt more pain if that were the case.

Well, she could only hope the bruise faded to nothing by Monday, which was highly unlikely, or she'd be caking on makeup. She *had* fallen, but Bonzo wasn't likely to believe any story she could probably concoct. He'd want to know *why* she fell. Lying wasn't a good forte of hers.

And Officer Crowl. What would he think?

Ha! Would he even care?

As she walked to the kitchen to grab a glass of wine, she told herself he would care—as a cop only. His look of concern today when she fell in front of his house hadn't been fake. Then he told her to leave.

Yeah, it would be in her best interest if she removed the evidence of the bruise to avoid any questions. She didn't feel like making up a story, or providing the real reason.

Grabbing the unopened box of wine from the pantry, she poured herself a full glass to the rim. She was in for a long night. Snagging the box in her left hand, she carried her glass in her right as she made her way to the living room. The box of wine took residence on her coffee table next to the open box of her jewelry supplies, then she plugged in her Christmas tree.

Sinking into the couch, she turned on some joyous music and let the spirit of the holiday fill her up. Something beautiful and magical to get her mind off of every horrible thing that happened today.

BEFORE HE COULD THINK about what he was doing, he raised his hand and knocked. He talked himself out of this at least a hundred times as he drove over to her house. Maybe more like two hundred times.

His mind refused to shut off. Theresa was all he thought about his entire shift. Which was probably why the drunken idiot he had to arrest for disorderly conduct at Hafferty's Bar managed to throw a fist at him. He avoided getting hit, because the dude *was* drunk and had lousy aim, but if his mind hadn't wandered, he would've never even had the opportunity to attempt anything.

Why wasn't Theresa answering her door?

He glanced at his wristwatch. "Because you're a dumbshit. She's probably asleep." His shift ended at ten o'clock, then he went home and changed before driving the long way to her house and trying to talk himself out of coming. It just hit eleven o'clock. Of course she was in bed. *I want to join her.*

Thoughts like that weren't going to get him anywhere. Turning around, his heart skipped a beat when he heard the swoosh of the door.

"Officer Crowl?" Her voice trembled. "Did something happen to my brother?"

He turned toward her and almost staggered back from the worry in her eyes. God, what an idiot. Why had he thought they had a moment? She thought he was knocking on her door so late at night because something might've happened to her brother. Here he was putting worry in her mind for no reason at all.

"I'm not here because of him." His eyes glanced down at his clothes. He had on a thick winter jacket, jeans visible with a pair of black and white tennis shoes. His state of wardrobe should've been clue enough he wasn't knocking on her door because of her brother.

When he looked back at her, she was biting her lip, the

worry gone and replaced with wariness. The hallway behind her was dark, as was the front stoop where they stood. Theresa needed a motion sensor light. It wasn't safe. He wanted to see her beautiful face without the shadows crawling over every inch.

"I wanted to make sure you're okay."

"Why wouldn't I be?"

"You fell today." His concern for her hadn't left his mind all day. Not his real reason for stopping by, but he had to grasp for something before he looked like more of a fool than he already did.

"I'm fine. Thanks for stopping by." The door started to slowly close.

"Wait." His hand stopped the door from shutting completely. *Think, idiot! Say something.* "You never gave me the necklace for my mother."

"Oh, of course. Umm..."

She really had no intention of inviting him in. Why should she? He never acted like a gentleman with her. He didn't warrant a good enough reason to be invited in, even if he had a lame excuse for stopping by so late at night.

He shouldn't want to be invited in. Coming here had been a mistake. But he couldn't help it. He wanted to feel happy for once, and anytime he was around Theresa, he felt that.

"I'm sorry, Ther—"

"Come on—"

They both stopped speaking, waiting for the other to finish their sentence.

Suddenly, her laughter filled the space, making the tension building between them slowly wither away like fog on a beautiful sunny morning.

"It's freezing outside. Come in while I grab the necklace."

She opened the door further and walked down the short hallway, obviously assuming he'd just follow. Which, of course, he did. He was finally inside like he'd wanted from the moment he decided to come over. He wasn't about to back down now. Although he should. He had no right to be in her home, wanting, wishing for things that he didn't deserve.

He closed the door and followed close behind her, which wasn't too hard as she took her time walking to the living room. Her steps were slow, but slightly uneven. When he eyed the box of wine on the coffee table and a half-consumed wineglass, he groaned internally at his lousy timing.

"Have you been drinking, Theresa?"

She whipped around so quickly she would have fallen to the floor if he hadn't grabbed her, one hand on her waist, the other on her back. Perfect position to pull her closer and snuggle against him. And he did a little. Her tiny steps didn't resist.

"Is it a crime to drink in your home by yourself?"

It took all of his strength not to close the distance to her lips. The glassiness of her eyes, which was easier to see now, and the smell of the sweet wine on her breath had him trying to maintain his control. Although he didn't drop his hands from her body.

"No."

"Then why does it matter if I'm drinking?" She scooted even closer. Not that he tried hard to stop her. "Why are you here?"

He already explained that. "The necklace."

She slapped her forehead. "Duh! Let me get it." She moved out of his embrace before he could stop her.

And what a bad idea it would've been to try and stop her. First, because he should've never showed up at her house. Second, because she was clearly drunk, or at least very tipsy. He'd never take advantage of her like that.

She circled the couch, bending in front of the coffee table as she rummaged through what looked like a fishing box. His body instantly reacted to the picture in front of him. Her round little ass wagging in the air had him wishing she had never touched a drop of wine tonight.

But because she had, he forced himself not to move a muscle.

Bolting upright, she snapped her fingers as she giggled. "It's not in there. It's in my coat pocket." She smiled, a sweet smile, as she pointed at him. "Be right back."

He watched her walk out of the room, her slow, lazy pace a serious turn on. Did she know the way her hips swayed side to side was reeling him in? Probably not. Theresa wasn't the kind of woman to flirt so blatantly.

A light sound of Christmas music filled the tiny living room space, although the sound was slightly muffled. He moved closer to the couch, eyeing her phone sitting close to the edge. Why wasn't she listening to music on the radio or a CD? Music never sounded pure and beautiful out of a tiny speakerphone.

Theresa clearly enjoyed the dark tonight because the living room was layered in darkness, besides the delightful tree lit up in the corner.

A Christmas tree.

He still didn't have one. As he thought about it, he never intended to put one up, but a plan started to form, one he should diminish in its tracks.

Theresa came back in the room with a small lacy drawstring bag. "I hope your mother likes it."

Aiden took the bag from her hand and opened the tiny pouch to reveal a sparkling yellow necklace that had three layers of beads. He poured it into his hand, eyeing the delicate design of light yellow beads patterned with darker yellow beads. It was simple, yet gorgeous. Like Theresa. He loved it, just because she made it. He had no doubt in his mind his mother would as well.

"It's gorgeous. She'll love it." He looked up, wanting so badly to kiss her breathless, but the glossiness in her eyes stopped any movement. "Will you help me find a Christmas tree tomorrow?"

She smiled, then laughed softly. "You don't need my help."

His resistance was slipping. A hand extended until he reached her cheek and brushed back a strand of her beautiful brown hair and tucked it behind her ear. "Maybe. But I want it."

In his crazy messed-up way, he was admitting he wanted her. Did she understand his mixed-up words?

"Officer Crowl—"

"Why do you always call me that?" It annoyed the hell out of him. "I want you to call me Aiden."

For a small second, she looked panicked. Or perhaps he interpreted it wrong. But he hadn't misinterpreted her silence. He was making her uncomfortable for some reason.

"Will you please help me tomorrow?"

"Sure."

That's all he needed to know. "I'll pick you up around noon. Have a good night, Theresa. Sorry for dropping in so late."

She nodded, but said nothing else as they walked to the

front door. He made sure he heard the lock click behind him before he headed to his vehicle.

He had a date.

Well, he thought so, anyway. Did Theresa see it like that?

Shit. He had to work tomorrow and he said he'd pick her up at noon. That wouldn't give him much time to hang out with her before his shift started at two. Would Chief Duncan give him the day off on such short notice?

Slamming his door shut, something close to a smile graced his face. The first real smile in the longest time. There was only one way to find out what the chief would say.

He just had to ask.

8

AIDEN HAD NEVER in his life requested the day off the same day he wanted it. Hell, since Cynthia died, he always asked for more time to work. He needed to keep his life busy, away from the moments where his mind could drift away.

Why was he doing this? Why was he pretending something good could happen between him and Theresa?

As the door swung open to a petite little girl with pigtails in her hair, he knew. Maybe he didn't deserve happiness, but he craved it. He yearned for a family of his own. A wife, a woman to love with all of his heart. A partner. Not someone who would control him and decide his every move.

Theresa just might be that person. He didn't know if he didn't give her the chance. So that's what he was doing.

"Hey, pipsqueak. Is the chief home?"

Laura smiled brightly, her cheeks blooming a soft shade of red. "Yep. Him and Grandpa are arguing about what Christmas movie we're going to watch. Come on in."

He stepped inside Chief Duncan's home, not straying from the foyer because he wanted to make this quick. Laura paused in her steps when she noticed he wasn't following her. "I'll just wait here."

"You know Dad won't mind if you stay for a cup of hot chocolate. Grandpa makes the best, and we're having that with some cookies while we watch a movie."

"That's the best offer I've had in a while, but I can't stay, pipsqueak. Maybe another time."

Her cheeks tinged an even darker shade of red. "That'd be awesome. Be right back."

He shook his head at her retreating back and chuckled. Laura was a sweet little girl. Since the moment he met her, he called her pipsqueak. Every time he did, she blushed a different shade of red.

Nerves, a very uncommon occurrence, attacked him as soon as Chief Duncan strolled into the foyer.

"Everything okay, Aiden? Not sure the last time you visited me here."

"Yeah. Everything's fine. I..." A breath left his mouth slowly. "I was wondering if I could have the day off. I already talked to O'Connor and he said he'd cover my shift. I wanted to make sure it was okay with you."

Chief Duncan puckered his brows briefly, then nodded. "Don't think I mean this offensively, but you never ask for time off. What's going on?"

Should he admit the real reason, or make something up? Theresa probably didn't even think it was a big deal. Not a date like he did. Maybe she'd back out when he tried to pick her up. Maybe she wouldn't even stay that long.

What the hell was he doing?

The chief placed a hand on his shoulder. "Aiden? Are you okay?"

"I...I don't know what I'm doing, Chief."

His hand fell away. "About what?"

Talk about awkward. It had to be for the chief as well, yet he didn't appear as if he found the conversation strange.

"I asked Theresa to come with me to get a Christmas tree." He shrugged. The simple statement said it all, which was confirmed when Chief Duncan smiled a little too brightly. What was with the smile?

"Enjoy your day off, Aiden. You deserve it."

Well, why did it feel like he didn't?

"You're sure? Because I—"

"If anyone deserves—and needs—a day off, it's you. You work too hard." Chief Duncan let loose a small sigh. "Sometimes you worry me. Trust me when I say I know how hard it is to lose someone you love dearly."

The chief was obviously talking about his mom, because besides that, he didn't suffer the loss of someone special in his life. If only the chief knew why he struggled with Cynthia's death. Nobody knew the real reason. He wasn't about to start explaining now. The chief could believe what he wanted.

"I'm fine, Chief. I promise. I appreciate you letting me have off on such short notice."

He said his goodbyes quickly and headed for his vehicle before the chief could twist any more emotions out of him. In the span of just a few minutes, he went from joy to sorrow to dread to happiness. It was like riding a damn roller coaster.

He made a quick call to O'Connor as he drove back home to let him know what the chief said. As soon as he walked back into his house, he went on a crazy cleaning frenzy. His house wasn't that messy, but he wanted it to look spotless before Theresa arrived. His life may be a complete cluster inside, but on the outside, he always made sure it looked in order. It took him less than thirty minutes to organize his house, considering it was already pretty spotless.

Glancing at the clock on the wall in the living room, he realized he only had twenty minutes before it was time to pick her up. He didn't even eat lunch. Did she? Should he have made something to eat for them? Would she expect food?

A tired hand ran down his face as another slew of torrential emotions flooded him. What the hell was he doing? Nothing would ever work out between them.

———

THERESA DABBED a little more concealer to her cheek, blending it in as best as she could. After another five minutes of trying to hide the bruise gracing her face, she sighed. He hadn't notice the bruise last night, although it would've been difficult since she had all the lights off. Hopefully he wouldn't notice it today either.

She couldn't figure out why he wanted her help with getting a Christmas tree. This was the second time he'd asked her for help. Did she appear that pathetic to him? Did he think she loved the holiday so much she'd do whatever when it came to Christmas festivities?

What did he really think? That's what she wanted to know.

He was up and down with her all the time. One minute acting like she was the rarest gem on Earth. The next like a piece of gum on the bottom of his shoe. Well, okay, maybe he wasn't that bad, but he could be such a grouch with her.

She poured herself a glass of water, hoping to soothe her rattled nerves some. Sleeping in this morning hadn't helped to reduce the hangover she had. The medicine she downed helped somewhat. The hot shower had done the trick. She stood under the warm spray for the longest time, just letting the heat calm her down. It also gave her time to think.

What crazy things had she said last night? She remembered most of it. It was the parts she couldn't quite recall that concerned her. By the time he stopped by, she had drank about half of the wine box. She hoped she didn't say anything too embarrassing, like, "Hey, do you like me? Because I have the hugest crush on you."

She downed the glass of water and then refilled her glass.

Wait! Maybe she misinterpreted his words. Here she was, patiently waiting for him to come pick her up, and he didn't intend to.

Setting the glass down gently on the counter, she smacked her forehead. "Idiot. He didn't ask you out. Your drunk-induced mind created that."

No big deal. How many times had she fantasized about him asking her out? Too many to count. She'd just chalk this in the too-bad-you-have-an-overactive-imagination category and move on. Maybe she'd take a bath. She had no other plans for the day and her head still pounded with a dull ache. A bath sounded soothing.

Swiping the glass of water from the counter, she drank it in one long swallow, then set the glass in the sink. As she headed for her bedroom to change, a loud knock sounded on her door.

With slow, hesitant steps, she walked to the door and jerked in surprise when she saw it was Officer Crowl standing on her doorstep. No. Aiden. She was somewhat positive he had asked her to stop calling him Officer Crowl. That it bothered him. Why?

Well, she wasn't going to ask.

He knocked again.

Oh, right. She should probably answer the door. Of course, in the light of day with no alcohol dulling her shyness, she was a little afraid to open the door. What should she say?

Gripping the handle a little too hard, she opened the door with what she hoped was a simple smile. Nothing that said *I'm so glad you're here. You make me so happy any time I see you.*

"Hi. You ready?"

She nodded, afraid to even respond with a hi back.

He snapped his fingers. "I almost forgot. Grab some boots, a hat, gloves, and a scarf. I don't want you to get cold getting the tree."

"Where are we going?"

His lip curled up slightly, almost resembling a smile. It made her weak in the knees, and so desperate to see a real smile on his face. What would it take to elicit a genuine smile from him?

"It's a surprise. Grab your stuff and I'll you meet in the car."

A surprise? Interesting. A strange giddiness flooded her. Maybe this wasn't a simple friend helping a friend. Could he see this as a date? She quickly grabbed her winter gear, exchanging her light knit mittens for a more heavy duty pair of gloves. Locking her door, she tried not to skip merrily to his car or show her excitement at spending the day with him.

As she shut the car door, her mood dipped. Spend the day with him? He worked on Sundays. Was that pathetic she knew his work schedule and they weren't even close friends?

"I guess we'll have to find a tree quickly. There won't be time to decorate it." Her face flamed with heat. "Not that I expected to help you decorate it. I wasn't implying that. I'm sure you don't want my help with that." She started to twist her hands fiercely. "You have to work later and—"

His hand covered hers that were coiled together in a tight ball. "I asked for the day off. I'd love your help decorating it."

"Oh."

Another small curling of his lip. "I could even show you how to string popcorn."

"Okay."

"Are you okay, Theresa? I don't want to make you feel uncomfortable."

She wouldn't say she was uncomfortable, even with his hand covering hers. She wished she would've waited to put on the gloves. She wanted to feel him skin to skin.

"Theresa?"

How did she explain how she felt right now? She couldn't even explain it to herself. He asked for the day off. To spend it with her.

Just. Wow.

"Office—Aiden..." She let out a slow breath as his features tightened into a scowl and just as quickly relaxed. So she remembered correctly. He didn't like it when she called him Officer Crowl. Good thing she caught herself. "What's going on here?"

He squeezed her hands. "I don't know. But I'd like to find out. I'm going to try hard not to act like a jackass. I'm sorry about that, by the way. What do you say?"

Wowza again. Was he admitting he wanted to start a relationship? Try to, anyway? Her mother never called her dumb. Might've said irresponsible a time or two, but never dumb.

"I think that's a great idea."

The smallest, sweetest smile emerged on his face. She almost melted into her seat at the sight of that glorious smile. It lit up his features so brightly, the striking lines of his jaw more prominent, the sparkle in his eyes more glittering. It just made him that much more handsome. He needed to smile more often.

"I think so, too." He cleared his throat as he backed out of her driveway. "Did you eat?"

"Umm..." Sadly, the thought of food earlier made her stomach cringe with a terrible urge to throw up. "Not really."

A low chuckle escaped. "Do you feel like eating before we hunt down a tree?"

Food was the furthest thing on her mind. Him, on the other hand, she'd devour in a second. "I can wait."

He nodded. "I'll whip something up after we find a tree."

"Sounds like a plan."

Another tiny smile appeared. "It sure does."

The trip to his house didn't take as long as the time she drove there. Of course, that could've been because she drove as slow as a snail, dreading and anticipating seeing him that day. When she stepped out of the vehicle and followed him to the front door with her stuff, she wondered why they were stopping at his house.

"Change into your boots and we'll go." He unlocked the front door and stepped to the side to let her in first.

"I don't think I need boots for Jeff's Tree Lot."

He closed the door and placed a hand on her back, pushing her forward lightly. "We're not getting a tree from there."

"Oh. Where are we going?"

He guided her to the dining room where her eyes followed his finger as he pointed to the sliding glass door that showed the beautiful view of his backyard. A light layer of snow covered the deck and the yard. A tiny shed stood to the left of the house. Beyond that was the woods. Everything looked so perfect and peaceful.

"We're going to walk through the woods until we find the perfect tree, and then we're going to chop it down."

"Seriously?"

His hand dropped from her back. He pulled out a chair for her to sit down and put her boots on. "Seriously. It'll be fun."

Yes, it will. She had no doubt about that. She had never walked through the woods to find a Christmas tree. The excitement to do it now was almost so overwhelming that she had to tie and retie her boots three times before she tied them correctly. Thankfully, Aiden had walked out of the room. When he walked back in, he had boots on his feet, a hat on his head, and large gloves covering his hands.

"Ready?"

She nodded and stood up, placing her hat, gloves, and scarf on. She followed him outside via the sliding door. He headed to the shed, pulling open the door without having to unlock it first. Not surprising. She knew some of her neighbors didn't even lock their doors when they left the house. It was a small town. Not much crime occurred. Out here, in the middle of nowhere, she imagined Aiden had no problems.

He grabbed an ax from the wall and closed the door. Then, without asking or warning, he grabbed her hand and started to walk. It was a funny grip, especially with both of them wearing such big gloves, but she almost wanted to squeal like a little girl whose crush just asked her to go steady. She couldn't help the sappy smile that touched her lips.

"So...how are the orders coming along?"

Orders? What orders? She had no clue what he was talking about, and honestly, she still couldn't get over the fact he asked her to come over, that he asked for the day off to spend time with her, and that he was holding her hand as they strolled through the woods looking for the perfect tree. To her, the day couldn't get any better. Unless he kissed her, of course.

"Is it too cold out? Do you want to head back?" His steps slowed as his hand fell away from hers.

She glanced at his hand, wondering why he disengaged. "No. I'm fine. I...uh...was trying to think of how the orders are coming along." That sounded so stupid. She didn't even know what the hell she just said.

His lips pressed together, as if he were trying not to laugh. "Yeah, and what'd you come up with?"

"That...they're coming along fine." She couldn't stop the laugh from escaping. Neither could he.

"Theresa. You have no idea what I'm talking about, do you?"

"That obvious, huh?" Turning her eyes to the snowy white ground, she could feel her cheeks turning red, and it was definitely not from the cold. "I'm a little nervous."

A roughened finger tilted her chin up. His eyes glimmered with laughter. "I was talking about your jewelry." He stepped closer as his finger fell away. "I'm a little nervous myself." He tossed the ax to the side and his gloved hands grasped her cheeks. "Maybe we should get the awkwardness out of the way."

"How are we going to do that?"

The biggest smile of the day brightened his face. "With a kiss, of course."

Then his lips were on hers, soothing her, calming her

rushing nerves. They were soft, tender. He took his time learning her lips before dipping his tongue in. That's when the flood of emotions tore down her anxiety. All her misgivings and worries fell away and all that remained was Aiden. Sweet, sometimes grumpy, Aiden.

She never wanted the kiss to end.

9

As soon as Aiden heard a soft moan from Theresa, he knew he needed to step away before he whisked her inside the house and forgot all about finding a tree. He had to move slowly with her. Not just for her, but for himself. He liked her in his arms. A lot. But the turbulent emotions of what happened with Cynthia lingered just on the surface, ruining the bliss he wanted to experience.

Pulling away reluctantly, his hands still grasping her face, he rested his forehead against hers. "Theresa..."

He didn't know how to finish that sentence. Maybe she knew what he was trying to say because she grabbed his jacket on the sides and squeezed. "Every time we kiss, it gets better and better. I don't feel awkward anymore."

Well, that wasn't necessarily what he was thinking, but he couldn't deny it was the truth. He moved away a fraction and pressed a light kiss to her lips. "Let's have some fun. I'm counting on you to pick out the best tree there is."

Her laughter sang in the woods, the sweet sound filling the area with warmth and happiness. "You do remember what my tree looks like, brown spots and whatnot?"

He let her go and picked up the ax, then grabbed her hand again as they started to walk. "It's a beautiful tree and you won't hear me saying otherwise."

She responded with the sweetest smile. He loved it every time she smiled, especially when her smiles were directed at him. Funny. Cynthia never smiled like that, especially with him. She always wore more of are-you-going-to-do-what-I-said sort of smirk. Although, to anyone else, it would've looked like a loving smile to her wonderful fiancé.

Squeezing Theresa's hand, just to remind himself of who stood next to him, he tried to push all thoughts of Cynthia out of his head. He had no reason to feel guilty. None whatsoever.

But he still did. Guilty as hell.

"Oh my gosh! Look, Aiden."

Her cry of surprise jolted him out his dark thoughts that might've ruined the day, forcing him to end it early and take her home. He followed her finger that pointed to the left and curled his lips into a tiny smile at the joy on her face over a deer. A stinking deer.

Pressing a finger to his lips, he slowly started to walk in that direction. The excitement increased in her eyes. She was giddy at seeing a simple deer. Cynthia wouldn't have glanced twice at it. Hell, she would've never walked into the woods with him to chop down a tree. A sharp remark about the cold weather and ruining her hair would've been more her style.

"It's so cute," Theresa whispered.

They stopped walking when the deer suddenly jerked its head in their direction, then took off running, prancing, and darting through the trees.

"That was amazing. I've never seen a deer so close."

Cynthia never—

Damn it! He needed to stop comparing them.

"Aiden?" Theresa turned to him. "Are you okay?"

He tried to remove the scowl he knew he had plastered on his face. "Yeah, of course. I'm glad you got to experience that. They walk through the backyard on occasion."

Her frown slowly morphed into a smile. "I bet that's just lovely to see when it happens."

"Yeah, it is." He pulled her hand so they could head back to their original path. "Let's find a tree."

He tried to shake off the gloom that surrounded him. Every time Theresa pointed out something new, even something as simple as how the snow looked resting on a branch, the sight a beautiful picture to her, it helped chase away his demons. But like the devil Cynthia had played in his life when she was alive, she still managed to do it in death. He couldn't erase her from his mind. Those treacherous thoughts would only lead him down one path. Making the day miserable for Theresa.

"Oh, look at that one. I like this one." She dropped his hand and pushed her feet through the snow to a tree that wasn't too big or too small.

It did have a few spots that could've been filled in a little more, making it look bare and sullen. Walking around it, he saw a branch low to the ground that twisted and angled itself in a funny way. It made the tree look strange from that side. It certainly wasn't a perfect tree. More like odd. They passed several trees that would've been great. Flawless and beautiful.

This one, more like weird and far from ideal.

"You don't like it?"

He glanced at her and shrugged. "We passed a few that didn't look...this has a few holes."

"It has character."

Theresa continued to gaze at the tree with such wonder. He looked at the tree again, trying to imagine what she was seeing.

"Not everything has to be perfect, Aiden." She blanched. "I'm not saying you want everything to be perfect." She let out a slow breath. "I'm just trying to say that just because something isn't what everyone else would choose doesn't mean it's not a good choice."

For a brief second, he almost thought Theresa was talking about herself. Did she think she wasn't perfect and he wouldn't want her because of it?

No. He was thinking way too deep right now. They were talking about a damn tree. If she liked this tree, then he would chop it down.

"I like it."

"You're frowning."

"I always frown."

Her giggles sliced through the tension that had started to form. It made him want to laugh with her, but his face was frozen, his entire body immobile, his feelings still crashing like heavy waves. He just wanted to feel happy without the darkness ripping it away every single time.

"We'll keep looking." Her laughter died, as did the beautiful smile on her face. She turned around to keep walking on the trail that would no doubt lead them to better looking trees.

That's not what he wanted. What he wanted was to see her smile again, and keep that smile without him ruining the moment. He always ruined it.

Without thinking about what he was doing, he reached down and cupped a handful of snow, pressing it into a small ball. Then he let it fly through the air. It hit her squarely on the neck. She immediately squealed and danced in a funny circle as she tried to scoop the snow out before it traveled underneath her jacket and down her back.

She was absolutely stunning, and so full of life. And utterly perfect.

He wanted her. So badly.

Icy cold hit his face. Specks of snow slowly drifted down, making him shiver from the snowball that hit him smack on the forehead. He wiped most of it away as his eyes sought her out. She stood by the trail, another snowball waiting in her hand. A smile gradually built into a beaming one. One that he hadn't had in the longest time. His face almost hurt from smiling so wide. But it felt damn good.

"It's war now. Prepare to be smothered in snowballs. I have excellent aim." He dove to the side as she threw her snowball and laughed.

He managed to tuck and roll, while scooping a ball up. He found her in his sights and tossed it her way. It hit her shoulder as she tried to duck.

Back and forth they went. Throwing snowball after snowball. He always managed to hit some part of her, and she would shriek in happy delight every time. He had to admit she had decent aim herself. She got him good plenty of times. A few in the chest, on the arm, and one that hit his neck area, a few snow chunks slithering down underneath his jacket.

Time to have some real fun. He charged her. Her eyes lit up with pleasure as she tried to dodge him, but he was too quick for her. Probably the many years of playing football. They fell to the ground. He made sure he landed first, tucking her into his arms, then rolled until she lay underneath him. She fit perfectly. In all the right places. He wanted to curse the cold, the snow, and the fact they were stuck out in the middle of the woods. He could take her right here and now, if not for that.

"Should I apologize for throwing that at you?" He smiled as he wiped a lock of hair away from the edge of her mouth.

"Not if it gets you to smile." Her eyes sparkled with delight. "I love when you smile." Her cheeks bloomed a deep red. "I love snowball fights. My brother and I used to have them all the time when we were kids. I just love playing in the snow."

"I guess that's why you had such great aim." His gloved hands grasped her cheeks as he pressed his body a little more firmly into her and kissed her breathless.

He could've kept the kiss going for longer. On and on and on. But he was ready to explode if he didn't have her soon, so he slowed it down and pulled away. Moving his hands away, he started to smile again, especially because she said she loved it when he did.

Just as swiftly, it turned into a fierce frown. His entire body went stiff. The rage flowed like a gushing geyser.

"Aiden? What's—"

"Who in the hell hit you?" His hand brushed the bruise on her cheek. His gloves, now wet from the snowball fight, made it easy to wipe off the makeup she clearly used to hide the evidence.

Her silence grated on his nerves, ramping his rage up even more.

"Damn it, Theresa, answer my question."

"It's noth—"

"Don't you dare say that." He leaned closer, his lips close to hers. "Someone hurt you. I won't let anyone hurt you. Tell me now."

"Nobody hit me. I fell."

"Yeah, sure. You fell. Don't lie to me."

"I'm not. I fell."

Just like that, his memories swamped him. She fell yesterday when she came to his house. He caused the bruise. He hurt her.

"Oh my God. I did this. I hurt you. I'm always hurting the ones I lo—" What the hell was he about to say? Love? He didn't love Theresa. But he cared for her far more than he should. "I'm so sorry."

He dropped his head into the crook of her neck, not even caring the cold, wet snow was hitting his face. He couldn't get any colder than he already was inside. The darkness was going to consume him soon. Why not now?

"This isn't your fault. I fell..." Her breath hitched. "It wasn't you."

Well, if it wasn't him, then who? He lifted his head. "Then tell me. Who hurt you?"

"I...it doesn't matter."

"It matters to me."

That was the honest to God's truth. She mattered. Probably more than he should let her. He wanted her so badly in his life that he should do them both a favor and end it before it started. Because if he lost her, he'd be so broken, nothing would ever fix him again.

10

HE LOOKED SO fierce as his warm body pressed her to the snowy ground. Not that she wanted to complain. She liked feeling him on top of her. If only they were in his house instead of outside lying on the cold ground.

"You better..." His voice became low and soft. "Theresa. Just tell me."

The look in his eyes didn't portray he wanted to know because he was a cop. His eyes said he wanted to know because he cared for her. That just made her not want to tell him even more. What would he do?

"Do you think by ignoring me I'll just forget it?"

"I just don't...it was nothing. Honest."

He scoffed. "Just like when your brother comes to your house drunk—" His face became hard as granite. "Did he do this?" The anger drifted out in heavy waves.

"No!" She couldn't let him think her brother had done this. She closed her eyes as she said, "I went to drop off his car and his roommate was the only one home. He grabbed my arm and when I pushed him to get away, I lost my balance and fell. Hit my cheek against the sidewalk. He didn't hit me."

His gloved hand brushed her cheek. "Open your eyes." She listened, popping them open slowly, surprised to see the anger gone and replaced with tenderness. "He still caused this. He still touched you."

"But—"

He put a finger to her lips. "And I know you. You just want me to let it go and do nothing about it. That's a really difficult thing to ask of me." He pulled his finger away, kissing her with an aching gentleness. "I also don't want to argue with you. I just want to enjoy this day. Because I haven't had this much fun in such a long time."

Since Cynthia. That wasn't hard for her to decipher.

"Don't try to hide something like this from me again."

"I wasn't trying—"

"Don't lie to me ever again either."

He had her there. She had tried to hide it from him.

"I'm sorry. Maybe you should just take me—"

He silenced her again, this time with his lips. She was more than okay with that. She didn't want to hear him say "Yeah, maybe I should take you home." Her eyes drifted closed as the kiss went from slow and tender to hard and passionate.

Then, suddenly, his lips disappeared. The loss of his sweet lips was heartbreaking. She couldn't explain why. Nor could she open her eyes, afraid to see what look would be in his eyes this time.

"Let's chop down this gorgeous tree. Then I'll feed you some lunch."

Her eyes opened wide at the tone in his voice. He actually sounded happy. The shimmer in his eyes confirmed that. What happened to his anger from moments before?

She doubted he would officially drop the subject. Maybe for now, but she knew he'd bring it up again.

"Unless you want me to take you home." He started to back away.

"No." Her quiet plea had him sinking back into her, his lips grazing hers once again.

"Then let's get chopping or I'm never going to stop kissing you."

She honestly wouldn't mind that. His kisses got sweeter and sweeter each time. He rolled to the side and stood up, offering his hand to help her. One quick yank and she stood close enough to feel his hot breath running down her spine with delicious intent. She wanted to say screw the tree and run to the house as fast as they could to the bedroom. The sharp glimmer in his eyes said he was thinking the same thing.

"You better stop looking at me like that, Theresa."

She tried to smile coyly. "Like what?"

His hand glided to her back, pulling her snug against him. "You know." He kissed her again, another soul-crushing kiss that melted her heart and made her feel like she was flying high up to the sky.

She felt the reluctance as he removed his lips and stepped away. Her body tingled from his kisses and her heart was now one big puddle of goo.

"Now stop looking at me like that. We have a tree to chop."

She went with another coy smile, then burst out laughing as he made a motion as if he was going to attack her with more kisses. A small chuckle left his lips as he bent down to where he had tossed the ax. It was the most beautiful sound in the world. She decided right then she would get him to smile and laugh so much today his face would hurt in the morning. Because every time he did, he became more alive. As if he were truly happy. Because there were times she didn't think he had any happiness left. Not since Cynthia died.

Her mood started to dip at that thought as he bent down to his knees and started swinging heavy chops to the bottom of the tree.

Would he ever love her as much as he loved Cynthia? Their love had been timeless. Everybody in the town knew they were the perfect couple. The kind of couple everyone strived to be. He had done everything for her. Always made her feel like the queen she deserved to be treated like.

Of course, Cynthia hadn't been the nicest person on the planet. She had a mean streak. Not as bad as Marybeth, but if something hadn't gone her way, watch out. But the devotion she always saw from Aiden, he had never seen the malice below the surface. He saw the queen before his eyes.

She wanted to feel like a queen. To have a man look at her with such love and devotion, like the most prized jewel in the world. Just like Cynthia.

How could she compete against her? Not that she should have to. Cynthia was gone. Never coming back. That was the problem. She couldn't compete with a dead woman with a memory so flawless.

Ha! What was she thinking? Love? He didn't love her. Probably wasn't even close.

But for her, she could feel the love for him slowly seeping in. Every time he flashed a rare smile, more and more love slipped in. And it scared her. Because only one person would get seriously hurt.

Her.

"What's the matter?" He started to stand up when she stopped him with one hand in the air.

"Nothing. I..." Her eyes darted to the tree that he had chopped halfway already, yet standing as if it were never touched. "I'm just wondering if I should stand on the other side. I don't want the tree to go toppling to the ground and get ruined or something."

His fierce frown said he didn't believe her lie, which it clearly was up until the point she said it. Now she wondered if it would get ruined.

"It'll be fine. It'll be heavy when it drops and I don't want you to get hurt any more than you already are." He turned back toward the tree and kept chopping away.

Way to go, Theresa. Just like that, she put a damper on the mood. He worried way too much about her getting hurt. She didn't think she'd even get a scratch from the tree, but by the rigidness in his posture, she didn't think he'd budge on his decision. If he didn't want her near as he hacked away at the tree, he wouldn't let her get near.

A slow smile grew. She liked this small protective streak of his. She never dated a guy who acted like this.

"Now you're smiling. Before you were frowning. What is it now?" The wrinkled lines in his forehead said he was still concerned, yet the glimmer in his eyes said he wanted to smile.

"Nothing."

"It's always something with you. It's never just nothing." The corner of his lip curled up.

"You look like a sexy lumberjack right now." Her hand whipped to her mouth for saying something so...flirty.

He chuckled, then focused his attention back to the tree.

Well, mission accomplished. She made him laugh once again.

So maybe she'd never be as perfect as Cynthia. She still managed to make him a little happy. Right now, that's what mattered. With that firmly in her mind, she let the worry of Cynthia drift away as he chopped the tree down with ease.

Besides the few times he stopped to make sure she was alright with her constant frowning then smiling, he chopped until the tree fell down with one big swoosh. The loud crunching sound as it hit the ground made her flinch. *I told you so* sat on the tip of her tongue, because she couldn't imagine based on the sound that some of the branches didn't break. The tree was far from perfect, but she didn't want him to have a really pathetic looking tree.

He went to stand by her and wrapped an arm around her shoulder, pulling her close. "That was a lot of work. My dad normally does the chopping. I never realized how sore my arms would be."

That surprised her. He made it look so easy. That wasn't the only thing that surprised her. "You never chopped a tree down with Cynthia?"

His entire body went stiff immediately, then his arm fell to his side. "No. I didn't."

Once more, she ruined the good mood surrounding them.

He didn't turn her way, his eyes transfixed on the tree. "I didn't think this through. I can't drag that back the entire way home." He swiveled slowly, the light in his eyes filled with darkness. "Let's go back home. You can warm up while I grab a sled and get this tree out of here."

All she could do was nod. She didn't want to argue with him. He clearly wanted to pretend to be happy when he was anything but.

Yeah, there was no way she could compete with a dead woman. She didn't even want to try. Because she had no clue how to compete with Cynthia. She hated when the light in his eyes died.

AIDEN TRIED to stop the dark emotions from taking over. He really did. Dragging the heavy tree from the middle of the woods to his back porch helped the gloomy mood dissipate slightly. The first sight of Theresa's beautiful smile as he opened the sliding door to grab a quick moment of warmth made some of the misery slip back in.

How could he be happy? How could this simple task make him feel more pleasure than he ever had with Cynthia? He felt guilty as hell.

"Do you need help getting it in the house? Let me—"

"I got it." With those abrupt parting words, he walked back outside. His fingers were frozen to the bone, even with heavy gloves on his hands. He could've used a few more minutes inside, but seeing her happy face was too much. What was he doing? Why had he invited her over? Should he be feeling happy when Cynthia was gone?

How would he get the tree inside without dragging it across the floor? Tons of pine needles would sprinkle all over his floor.

Minutes passed. Maybe only seconds. He didn't know how long he stood there, his eyes zoning out as he stared at the tree, not really thinking about how to get it inside. Just staring.

When a soft hand landed on his shoulder, he wanted to forget about the tree, go inside, and do things he shouldn't even contemplate, let alone fantasize about.

"Did I do something wrong? Maybe I—"

He clamped a gloved hand over hers as he turned toward her. "You didn't do anything wrong."

"Why does it feel like it? If I said something—"

"You didn't say anything wrong."

Things said about Cynthia shouldn't bother him so much. That wasn't on her. It was on him.

She smiled gingerly. "Can you stop interrupting me?"

He wanted to match her smile. He wanted to pull her into his arms and kiss her breathless. "I can't help it." Kissing her would be a dangerous thing right now so close to the house, but he couldn't resist wrapping an arm around her waist and pulling her closer. "You get this cute little frown when I do." A corner of his lip curled up. "Not that I'm doing it on purpose or anything."

The air became thick and heavy with desire. Even with the cold, sharp wind biting into their faces, he could feel the passion filling up between them.

But nothing could happen. Not yet, anyway. He should take it slow. What was he thinking? Slow? He shouldn't be thinking like that at all.

Letting his arm drop, he took a step back before his common sense fled and he whisked her inside to his bedroom. His gaze fell on the tree. Then he turned to her with a silly grin, hoping to clear away the gloomy mood that was slowly eating him alive.

"Maybe I do need a little help."

"Yeah, maybe." She chuckled as she positioned herself at one end of the tree as he moved to the other.

"Wait. I pulled out the tree stand, but I didn't situate it where I wanted it. We should figure this out before we drag the tree inside." He laughed, somewhat lamely, because he was clearly not prepared for any of this.

"I set it near the corner of the living room, close to the fireplace. You're lucky you have a fireplace. It will make everything look so beautiful."

She was the beautiful one. He wanted to say that with other tender comments.

Cynthia's face flashed before his eyes. He turned his head to the ground, blowing out a deep breath.

"That was highly inappropriate of me. I shouldn't have moved it. I'm sorry."

His eyes whipped to her gorgeous face, cursing himself inside for putting the sad frown on her face. "No. I appreciate it. That's a great spot." He tried to shake off the bad thoughts one more time and lifted his end. "Let's get this puppy inside."

She offered him a weak smile and grabbed her end. Within less than twenty minutes, they had the tree inside, in its stand, and situated just right in the corner of his living room. His house was starting to look like he wanted to enjoy the holiday this year. He did. Sort of. As long as he had Theresa to share it with. Otherwise, the holiday would feel lonesome and bare. He really didn't want to feel that way.

Sure, he had his family to spend the holidays with. His mom loved Christmas. But it wasn't the same. He didn't get a giddy, silly feeling in the pit of his stomach when his mom smiled. Only Theresa managed to do that.

His mom had tons of questions this morning when he stopped by her house to ask for some decorations. When Cynthia died, he donated most of her stuff—most of the Christmas decorations were hers—to the surrounding shelters and donation centers. All of her other belongings, he gave to her family. She thought she had picked out nice, elegant stuff to fill their home with joy. Every time he looked at it, he saw snooty and stuck up instead. He hated it all.

When he walked into Theresa's house, her simple things had filled his heart with the holiday spirit. With a little joy.

His mother gave him a few ornaments for the tree, the ones he made himself growing up. She also gave him an extra tree stand they had and one set of lights, which wasn't enough to cover a tree. He had to stop at the local hardware store that also sold Christmas decorations and stock up on everything else he needed. Bernie, the owner, had given him a strange look, but smiled as he rang everything up.

It probably was odd of him buying tons of Christmas supplies. Last year had been the first time he'd spent Christmas alone. Mostly alone. He made an appearance at his parents' house, for their sake. The rest of the time, he wallowed in his self-pity and asked Chief Duncan for more hours to work.

Decorations? He didn't bother with something he deemed trivial. Not to mention, he didn't own any decorations.

Now he did. Now he found the task fun and delightful. He had Theresa's help to make it look as wonderful as her house.

"It looks great."

He glanced at her. She stood close to him, her hands clasped together in front of her with an adorable smile on her face. He agreed. It looked great, and so did she.

"It'll look even better after we decorate it. I'm starving, though. How about you?"

Her face turned a bright red as she nodded. "I hope you're not upset. I felt weird just waiting in your house doing nothing. That's why I moved the tree stand, and I also made some sandwiches. I hope that wasn't too forward of me."

He broke her hands apart and slid his fingers to intertwine with hers. "That was thoughtful of you. I didn't think this day through." He pulled her closer. "I feel like I keep mucking everything up. Saying things...ruining the mood." He turned his head down, yet squeezed her hands for strength. "I want you, Theresa. You fill me with happiness when I feel like I don't deserve any. I really like the feeling you give me. I just...I don't know how good I'm going to be at a relationship." He slowly lifted his head, meeting her gaze. "I want to try, though." He grinned. "I hope that wasn't too forward of me."

She bit her bottom lip as a tender smile graced her face. "That is the sweetest thing anyone's ever said to me."

"I find that hard to believe."

"Believe it. You think you're not going to be good in a relationship. I'm a novice. I rarely date. I've never been in a serious relationship like you—" She looked appalled. "I don't mean to bring her up. I know how much she meant to you, and here I am, making you feel horrible."

Something must've flashed on his face for her to say that. Maybe she saw sadness, as if he missed Cynthia. He'd call it more like guilt.

Cynthia liked to control him when she was alive. He'd be damned if she continued to control him in death. It was time to start pushing those damaging thoughts of her out of his mind and keep them out. It'd take all the strength he could muster, but he'd do it. Especially right now.

He dropped her hands and grasped her face as his mouth connected with hers. Her lips opened to him, moaning delicately. She moved closer, molding to his body. His hands brushed across her cheeks and through her hair, then made a smooth path down her arms and to her waist. A delicious shiver rushed through her, giving him the courage to keep moving this moment forward. He wanted her. Badly. He was going to have her. No more messing around and skirting his feelings.

He cupped her ass and lifted her. Theresa took the cue and wrapped her legs around his waist. Her body felt perfect against him.

Breaking the kiss, he sent a trail of kisses from her mouth to her ear, where he lightly nibbled before whispering, "Can I show you my bedroom? I don't think I gave you the full tour of my house."

Her hot breath against his neck teased him mercifully. "I'd love a tour."

He planted a kiss in response and started to walk out of the living room. She kept her head tucked between his neck and shoulder. She said she hadn't been in a serious relationship and rarely dated, but he could feel her nerves shining through.

As he walked into his room, he bypassed the light. The sun was shining brightly through his window. He opened the curtains every morning, enjoying the scenery and the sunlight that poured through. He liked to imagine it could fill up the parts of him that were so dark and empty. Most days, it failed.

He laid her on the edge of the bed, his hard arousal pressed tightly against her body, and leaned over her with his lips close to hers.

"Do you want this? We can stop now and just go decorate the tree." He brushed her hair back. "You said...you haven't dated much. Have you ever..." Wow. This conversation was more difficult to talk about than he realized. He felt like an idiot. But he needed to know. He'd never pressure her into something she wasn't ready for. Hell, he wasn't sure he was ready to be with another woman.

Her eyes were lit up with pleasure. Her mouth poised with a sweet smile. Her body felt made for his body.

He might not be ready, but he wanted her so badly it just didn't matter. Theresa always made him feel lighter, more free. If he was going to move forward with a woman, it'd be with this beautiful woman in his arms.

HE WANTED to know if she was a virgin. Talk about embarrassing, but oh so necessary to know. She was an adult. She could have an adult conversation, especially if they were about to have sex.

Sex with Aiden. Yes, please.

She giggled as that thought rolled through her mind.

His lip curled into a tiny grin. "Something funny?"

"No. I want this to happen...and I'm trying to remind myself I can have this conversation." She chuckled again, even though it wasn't funny. It was a very serious question he attempted to ask. She appreciated that he thought to have this talk before going any further. "I've done this before." Her eyes turned away because now she was embarrassed. "It's been a while." A pause. "A long while."

A gentle hand moved her chin so she was looking directly into his eyes once more. "Me, too. I haven't been with anyone since...and even before she...it's been a very long time for me, too."

His eyes clouded over with sadness. She had done it again. Or maybe he loved Cynthia so much he couldn't help but think about her all the time. Did he even want to do this? Who would he think about? Her or Cynthia?

"Maybe we should..."

His jaw clenched and the muscles in his cheek twitched like crazy. "I want this. I want you. Nobody but you. I...shit." He pushed away from her and walked out of the room.

Well, that went from passionate to ice-cold within less than five minutes. How had it gone so wrong? Maybe it was never meant to go right. He just loved Cynthia too much to want her.

She slowly sat up and glanced around his room. A very

sparse room. A bed, a dresser, and the curtains on the windows. That was it. No pictures. No knickknacks. No nightstand. Nothing. Strange.

His house was clean and put together well. He had pictures of his family out in the living room. So why did his bedroom look so bare?

It's not like she was going to ask. She didn't even want to ask for a ride home. She wished she lived within walking distance. It would make things easier. Because right now, she couldn't even find the nerve to stand up and go find him.

What a coward.

She bent her head, fiddling with her fingers, trying to forge the courage to get up and walk out of his room.

"I'm ten kinds of an idiot. I told you I don't know what the hell I'm doing here."

Her head jerked up to see Aiden standing in the doorway. His eyes portrayed so much agony. She had no idea how to erase that.

"I'm sorry I screwed it up." She shrugged, unsure of how else to apologize.

He closed his eyes as he shook his head, then fixed his gaze on her as he stalked to her and knelt down. He grasped her cheeks within his hands. "You didn't do anything wrong. I did. I mucked this up."

"But—"

He pulled her toward him and kissed her. A long, deep kiss that contrasted with his sour mood. Did he or did he not want her? She was so confused. The kiss continued to confuse her as it wrapped her into a tight cocoon of bliss. His lips slowed, bringing the kiss to an end.

Leaning his forehead against hers, he whispered, "I can't talk about what I want to. It's hard. But I want you to know that you didn't do anything wrong. I want you and only you.

Although I ruined the mood. Why don't we decorate the tree, eat lunch, and see what happens. What do you say? I..." He pressed his lips lightly to hers. "I'm not ready for you to leave."

"I don't want to leave either. If you're sure you still want me here, I'd love to decorate the tree."

"I do." He backed away slowly and stood up, then held his hand out. "The tree won't look good without your magical touch." He produced a small grin.

She could still see the melancholy in his eyes, but she appreciated the effort of his grin. His smiles always made her stomach flip flop like crazy. Offering a small smile in return, she took his hand and followed him out of the room.

Yeah, the moment was ruined. It didn't mean the moment couldn't be revived later. Who knew what would happen after they ate and decorated the tree. Even if she didn't make it back to his bedroom, she was happy. She didn't want to rush him into anything.

When they finally had sex, if they made it that far, she only wanted one thing on his mind.

Her.

11

"Come on. Close your eyes."

Theresa couldn't suppress a smile as she connected with Aiden's gaze where he stood near the outlet close to the tree.

"I want to see it lit up."

He shook his head. "Me, too. So close your eyes. I want it to be a surprise." A slow delicious grin grew. "Please."

Enjoying this playful side of him, she obeyed. She could hear rustling around as if he was shuffling things near the tree instead of just plugging it in.

The air had been tense between them when they walked out of his bedroom. Eating their sandwiches at the dining room table had gradually brought them back to an easy camaraderie. They talked about superficial stuff, things that wouldn't conjure memories of Cynthia. At least, she hoped so. He never produced the same ache in his eyes, indicating she didn't. That was a very good thing. She hated when he got that look in his eyes.

After a quick lunch, they started decorating the tree. Surprisingly, the day went from awkward to easygoing to comfortable to so much fun, as if it were a ritual. Something they did every single year. He strung the lights, goofing around so much that he got dizzy from walking around the tree so many times. Together, they hung the ornaments, taking their time to hang each one. Some of the ornaments were handmade and she insisted hearing the story behind each one.

Some were wooden, half painted with care, and the other half looked painted by a child: a Christmas tree, a sled, a dog, a cat, a football, and a star. Some were metal. Some were glass balls with tiny hand prints created into a beautiful winter scene. Each ornament had a story that she devoured and soaked into her memory as he explained why they were special.

Oh, and she knew they were special even as he shrugged it off as no big deal. She could see it in his eyes. They shimmered with adoration as he held them in his hand, warmly rubbing the top with his thumb. She wanted to know why he played it off as no big deal. His memories were important. Didn't he know that? Every time he finished a story, he handed the ornaments to her to hang on the tree.

When they finished decorating the tree, they hung a few more decorations that he said he bought that morning. The items he purchased weren't enough to fill his house completely of the Christmas spirit, but it helped. As they walked around, placing a few holiday knickknacks here and there, she realized the rest of his house was almost as bare as his bedroom. Oh, he had a few pictures of his parents on the walls, in addition to other family members, but mementos? She didn't see much. She had little knickknacks scattered all around her house. Maybe he just wasn't that kind of person. But she had to admit, the few things they placed around made her feel like the house actually felt like a home, not just another dwelling.

Of course, she hadn't said any of that. Not only would it have dropped the mood back to dangerous levels, she didn't think he'd appreciate her judging him like that. Not that she was judging him badly. She just found it odd, and she didn't want him to feel bad.

"Can I open my eyes yet?"

A warm pair of hands covered her eyes. His hot breath rushed down her spine in delicious tingles as he whispered close to her ear, "Impatient much? I want this to be perfect."

"It already is." Her voice tumbled out in a whisper, charging the intimate moment even more. She could feel the electric energy of desire surge to life once again between them. It had slowly been charging since they first started to decorate.

A light kiss touched her neck, then his hands disappeared. "You can open your eyes."

Theresa's eyes popped open and she gasped in wonder.

Gorgeous.

Everything was just...

She couldn't find the words. Beyond gorgeous.

The tree stood tall and proud in the corner of the living room with twinkling colorful lights arranged flawlessly on the branches. Ornaments hung here and there, no particular rhyme or reason, but just right to create a picture that glittered with perfection. Sitting on top was a white angel with feathery wings and a golden halo above her head. She looked as if she were staring directly at Theresa, granting her a Christmas wish. One she wished for in that exact moment. To spend the holiday with Aiden by her side. To have a merry Christmas filled with fun and laughter. That's all she wanted for Christmas this year. That didn't sound like much to ask for.

Her eyes drifted to the floor. A beautiful red tree skirt

with sparkling snowflakes was wrapped around the bottom of the tree. Sitting delicately in the middle was a bright red and green present with a red bow on top of it.

"That's for you, you know. I saw it today and I couldn't resist." He grabbed her hand and pressed a light kiss to it. "I'd love it if you came over on Christmas Day."

Wow! The angel already granted her wish. That was quick.

"I'd love to. The tree is beautiful."

His eyes twinkled with delight as he leaned closer. "You're beautiful." His lips touched hers. Light and sweet, but enough to tell her how much he meant what he said. He backed away, his hand still clasped with hers as they both looked at the tree again.

"Thanks for helping me today. I don't think it would've turned out half as beautiful as this if you wouldn't have."

"I had so much fun." Her eyes glossed to his fireplace. No fire crackled in the background, but a string of white lights graced the mantel with a few wooden blocks that said MERRY CHRISTMAS.

"You need some stockings. A fireplace needs stockings."

"You're right. I'll add that to my list." His eyes trailed to the sliding door and the dark night outside. "It's later than I realized and you have to work early tomorrow. I should get you home." He looked at her. "I really do appreciate you helping me."

"Anytime."

Definitely, anytime. Now that she knew what fun and joy she had with Aiden, she wanted to do it all the time. But would she? Sure, he invited her over for Christmas Day, but what were they? How did she define them? Friends? A couple?

As they picked up their mess and rustled her things

together, she decided she didn't have the nerve to ask. She'd just take one day at a time. Christmas wasn't too far away. He wanted to spend it with her. That was enough.

And he already bought her a present. What in the world could he have bought her?

What in the world should she buy him?

When they pulled into her driveway, she expected a quick goodbye. Maybe even a kiss. Instead, she found him walking her to the door, waiting patiently as she struggled to get the key in the lock.

Her nerves were unleashing full force. Did he want to come in? Was he just being gentlemanly walking her to the door? Was it the cop in him that wanted to make sure she made it inside safely?

She didn't care what the reason was, but it made her nervous enough that she couldn't get the key in the hole until the third try.

Finally twisting it unlocked, she pushed the door open a crack and then turned around. His eyes glittered brightly.

"You need a sensor light. It's dark out. It's not safe. Anyone could come up behind you as you're trying to unlock the door."

She swallowed, unsure whether he was purposely trying to scare her. "I only rent. I'd have to call my landlord. It's not a big deal. I'm usually home before it's dark."

His arm snagged around her waist and pulled her closer, his lips a breath away. "It is a big deal. I want you to be safe, regardless if you rarely come home late. Call your landlord tomorrow."

"Okay," she whispered breathlessly. Who was she to argue when he looked at her like he wanted to eat her up for dessert. Ha! The main course, actually. They didn't eat supper yet.

"Theresa," he softly murmured before he claimed her lips. The kiss was deep and thorough. It spoke of the hunger that had been slowly simmering and raging between them all day. He broke the kiss, breathing heavily.

What did she have to lose? She couldn't screw up any more than she had this afternoon. "Would you like to come in for a little bit? A tour of my bedroom, perhaps?"

"I thought you'd never offer."

NERVOUS DIDN'T BEGIN to describe how he felt. He followed Theresa inside, locked the door, hung their jackets up in the hallway closet, then grabbed her into his arms and fumbled his way to her bedroom.

Now he was laying the most beautiful woman in the world down onto the bed, and the nerves were swimming through his veins like a bunch of piranhas on a rampage. Sex. This was just sex.

Hell, who was he kidding? This moment was more than just sex. At least, on his part. He sensed Theresa felt the same thing. For that reason, he should shove away from her and run like hell. He had already done that once today, regretting it the exact moment he had. There'd be no regretting this moment.

The one fact he couldn't erase, or argue with, was that it had been one of the best days of his life. Honestly, that was sad and slightly pitiful. Chopping down a tree and putting Christmas decorations up, as most people did, shouldn't be considered one of the best days of his life. But it was.

He had a strong feeling he wanted to do it every single year with her. Just as they had done this year. Find a tree, chop it down, put it up, then take their time decorating it with fun and laughter and stories of beautiful memories. Each year, they could add more stories. Well, first, they had to make some ornaments together. He couldn't wait to create memories with her.

He kissed her briefly, his hands lingering on her cheeks before he pressed them to the bed and leaned away. "Are you sure this is what you want?" He hated to ask the question, but he needed to be sure. He'd never rush her into anything she didn't want.

Her hands shuffled to the hem of his shirt and dragged it upwards. "Yes."

He helped her take his shirt off, then went about making hers disappear. She wore a red lacy bra that had him producing the biggest, widest grin of the night. "Did you wear this for me?" A finger traced the outline of her bra.

She inhaled softly as her eyes dilated with pleasure. "Maybe. I like red. It's Christmassy."

He bent down, brushing part of the bra to the side to suck on her hard nipple. "I think I love red." He slid down until his hands were on the snap of her jeans. "Is it a matching set?"

Her eyes twinkled with mischief as she shrugged. "Maybe."

He quickly undid her jeans and slid them off, appreciating the beauty lying before him. It *was* a matching set. A pair of tantalizing red lace panties sparkled back, begging him to remove them as well. "Perfection. Every inch of you."

Before he touched her again, knowing he'd probably lose control, he removed all of his clothes. He shuffled through his wallet and tossed a condom on the bed. Theresa's eyes followed the movement, then glanced back at him, a smile still gracing her face.

He panicked for about half a second that she had

changed her mind at eyeing the condom. Nope. If anything, the desire spreading across her face increased expo- nentially.

He moved closer to her, his hard erection nestled perfectly between her legs, just waiting for his chance. "Move to the middle of the bed...please."

She did as he asked and he silently followed her like an animal on the prowl. She rested her head onto a fluffy pillow with a dark green pillowcase and spread her arms out wide.

"Red and green before me. It's almost like I get to unwrap a present." He slid over her, relaxing on top of her. He dropped his lips to hers. "Best present ever."

She giggled into his mouth as her arms came around him. The kiss went on as time slowed to a stop, even as his body begged to just dive in. Claim her. Possess her. Own her. But he held his control. A little part in his brain made him wonder if he was doing that on purpose. That maybe he was more afraid than he wanted to admit. What would happen after he took the plunge? Consumed her from head to toe?

More happiness waiting for him, perhaps.

That's what scared the living daylights out of him.

Pushing all nasty thoughts away as best as he could, he pulled away from her sweet lips and removed her bra and panties while placing tiny kisses around each area as he did. Theresa said nothing, but the way her body moved so eroti- cally told him how much she enjoyed everything. Arching this way. Bending that way. Each tiny movement from her had him aching for the ultimate prize. He wanted to place a few more kisses up and down her body, but it had been so long. So, so long. He was officially sick of waiting.

He grabbed the condom, donned it on, and positioned himself, but not before he attacked her lips in another soul-crushing kiss. She moaned, wrapping her arms tightly around him. This moment, everything about today, felt right. As if she'd been destined to be in his arms from the beginning.

"Are you sure about this?" He pulled his head back so he could read her expression.

She looked somewhat shocked by the question. "Are you? Because I was sure when I asked you to come inside."

His answer spoke louder than any words he could've responded with. He slid inside her with ease, pausing for a few seconds. "Perfection. In every way," he whispered against her lips before he claimed her mouth once more.

They moved slowly and tenderly. They weren't in a rush. He wanted to savor every moment of this. Being with her was as if every little piece of him that had turned dark was finally renewed with her lightness. He couldn't hold back. He absorbed every part of her beauty and passion, each tiny movement she made, as he slid in and out. It all filled him with so much happiness, he wanted to explode into complete bliss.

Perhaps it was those thoughts that made him thrust a little faster, their kisses turning hotter. Theresa matched his pace, snaking her arms down his back and to his ass where she held on tightly. The soft touch of her hands drove him crazy, making him pump even faster. Her sweet, erotic moans filled the room.

He broke the kiss, sending little tiny kisses to her neck as they moved effortlessly together.

"Oh, I'm so close, Aiden. Please..."

His lips attached to her shoulder as her quiet pleas soared through every part of his soul. He made her feel like this. Glorious. Beautiful. Begging for more. He loved it.

Shit. He loved her.

He pumped hard and fierce, her moans increasing in volume as she tensed beneath him. Her orgasm triggered his own. He held her tightly as all the love she just unleashed from him flowed through every part of him, his lips still attached tightly to her shoulder.

After what felt like ages, he let go, pressing tiny kisses up her neck to her ear. "Absolute perfection."

A soft sigh. "Did you have more than one condom in your wallet?"

He chuckled as he raised his head. "Only the one. You don't have any?"

Her faced bloomed a deep red. "Not something I keep in stock."

"I got an idea." He kissed her, then lifted himself up and scooted off the bed and plucked the condom off. "Where's your bathroom?"

"Right across the hall."

He stood up and winked. "I feel dirty."

She looked at him confused.

"Don't you?" He winked again, to show her he was teasing, playing around. He felt wonderful. Alive and free. He wasn't ready to leave or to stop touching her. A shower of fun sounded like a great plan.

Recognition of what he wanted finally appeared on her face. "Yes, I do believe I feel dirty." She rolled to her hands and knees and slowly crawled to the edge of the bed. "I feel very, very dirty."

It's like he unleashed a sex vixen. He loved it.

He loved her.

Shit. Loving her was the worst thing he could possibly do. He pushed all those thoughts out of his mind as he grinned deviously. "Come on, dirty girl. It's shower time."

THE INSISTENT BEEPING sound was ruining her good sleep. She slapped a hand to the alarm clock, hoping she hit the right button. The sound stopped, so she figured she hit something right. Maybe she hit the sleep button. It wouldn't be the first time.

Stretching like a cat, her arms reached high. Her first clue that she was alone was the empty air her hand hit instead of a warm body. Opening her eyes, she took a peek to the right where Aiden had been lying before she closed her eyes last night. Empty.

Her eyes glided to the floor looking for his clothes. Empty.

Bolting upright, she walked around her house naked, searching for him. Empty.

He left without a word goodbye. Just to be safe, even though she knew he wouldn't be hiding in a closet or something, she peeked out the window to see if his car sat in the driveway. Empty.

He really left.

Last night had been amazing. Beyond amazing. She'd had sex before. Those few times had been tame compared to what Aiden showed her. He only had the one condom, so creativity had been called for. They enjoyed a shower, playing, washing each other as if they'd been doing it for years. When they'd stepped out, warm and sated from not only the steam filling the bathroom but from the heat building between them, he carried her back to the bedroom and proceeded to kiss and touch her everywhere. She swore she could still feel his lips lingering on parts of her body. He didn't miss a spot.

Of course, she wanted to have fun, touching and

caressing and kissing him in spots she'd never done with a man before. At first she worried she was doing it all wrong, but by the moans and soft growls that left his mouth, she did it all perfectly.

Perfection.

Yeah, he said that a few times last night. Oh, so right. Every moment had been pure perfection. So why had he left without saying goodbye?

Trying not to worry about that particular question, she took a shower and almost slipped on the bathroom floor when she saw the huge hickey on her shoulder after she wiped the steam from the mirror.

She brushed a finger across it, igniting the memory when they made love and how his mouth had attached to her. He branded her. Marked her.

She smiled at the thought. When she walked into her room to dress for work, eyeing the empty bed, those worrying thoughts rolled back in. Why had he left?

The day dragged by. Work was work. Busy for the breakfast rush, slow waiting for lunch, and busy again when lunch finally arrived. She couldn't resist glancing at the clock as it slowly ticked to two o'clock. Bonzo kept asking her if she was alright. Maybe he saw her nervous energy. Not once had she received a call from Aiden, or a visit. Although, he never visited her before his shift. But last night...

She just wanted to see him. To know they were...what? A couple? Going to see each other again? Well, of course they were. He invited her over for Christmas. They had to help decorate for the annual Christmas party on Friday. She'd see him again. Maybe even tonight.

When two o'clock came and went, she started to worry. Then three o'clock came and went. By four, she knew something was wrong. He didn't come in for his coffee. He always came in.

Last night was amazing. Perfection, something he'd said himself. Why was he ignoring her?

She nearly jumped when the bell above the door rang with merry. She steeled her features as she turned around to see who stepped in.

Chief Duncan.

That's not who she wanted to walk in. At all.

"Hi, Theresa. I'll have a wonderful cup of coffee."

"You know it's not wonderful. I don't know why you all pretend with me." She poured him a cup, instantly hating herself for snapping at the chief like that. So what if Aiden hadn't come in for his coffee. So what if he left without a goodbye. It didn't mean she should take out her frustrations on other people.

She set the coffee on the counter and glanced at the chief, disliking the concern in his eyes.

"Everything okay, Theresa?"

"I'm fine."

He looked like he wanted to say more. Instead, he smiled, paid for his coffee, and left.

As she walked home, the blistering cold barely registered. She could only think one thing. She was nothing more than a silly conquest for Aiden. Boy, she had given in easily.

Damn him. And damn her for falling so easily into his arms.

12

AIDEN TOOK a deep breath before he knocked on the chief's door. He hated being called to his office. In fact, he couldn't ever recall being summoned to the office. Maybe that's why he was panicking inside like a high school student being sent to the principal's office.

"Come on in, Aiden. Have a seat. Close the door, please."

He backtracked to close the door, detesting the visit more and more. Why did he have to close the door? That just tipped the scale from slightly worrisome to downright panicky. It signified he wanted privacy. He didn't want anyone else to hear what he had to say.

What did he have to say? He wasn't sure he wanted to know as he took a seat in one of the two plush chairs in front of the chief's desk.

His life had become complete shit. He was almost afraid it was worse than when he lost Cynthia. Losing Theresa seemed ten times, no, a hundred times worse. She—

Was not his concern. He needed to remember that.

"What's up, Chief?"

Chief Duncan sat in his chair, no decent expression

for him to decipher. He couldn't stand the silence. Silence made him think, and thinking was bad. The past few days, all he did was think. He hated every minute of it. Now he hated every second. The chief called him into the office for a reason. He wanted to know the reason and move on.

"Is everything okay?"

He swallowed hard. "I'm fine."

"You know who else said that to me a few days ago?" He leaned forward, resting his elbows on the desk. "Theresa." His eyes narrowed. "I didn't believe her. And I don't believe you either."

It took every ounce of his control and strength not to stand up and walk out. If he did that, he'd most likely lose his job, because he didn't think he'd have the courage to walk back in. He loved his job too much to lose it.

But he couldn't—didn't want to—talk about Theresa. He didn't want to hear how she wasn't fine. Because he's the one who made her not fine.

He chose not to say anything as Chief Duncan stared at him hard. The chief was easy going. He'd never seen this look from him before, and it sort of scared him. Maybe he would be losing his job today. Wait. Could he lose his job for breaking Theresa's heart?

Did he even break her heart?

Well, that was a dumb question. Of course he had. He broke his own heart. That night…was everything. He had never felt anything so powerful before. If he felt it, then she had to have, too.

"What happened between you and Theresa?"

"I'm not sure what—"

"Don't bullshit me, Aiden." The muscle in his cheek started to twitch. "Everything is not okay." He paused. "And it hasn't been for a long time. You were back to work pretty quickly after Cynthia died—"

"I'm not talking about her." He stood up.

Surprisingly, the chief stood up as well, his expression still hard and foreboding. "Sit. Down. You're going to talk. If not with me, then somebody else. You need to talk about it. I should've never let you come back to work as quickly as you did. I've never had a problem with you on the job, but clearly, your personal life isn't doing so great and that can transfer to the job."

Aiden glared back. He didn't want to sit. He didn't want to talk. He didn't want to do a damn thing but run.

"Sit down." The expression on the chief's face softened. "I've been in the diner every day this week, and every day Theresa looks worse. Just tell me what happened. Because, as I look at you, I can see you're not doing any better. Please, Aiden, talk to me."

He tried to gulp in a breath of air, yet he was afraid to breathe for fear the panic would take over. He sank into the chair and shoved his head between his legs as a panic attack threatened to overwhelm him. His chest constricted as he tried to gulp in a breath of air. Trying to concentrate on that simple task for several long seconds, he could feel his body start to relax in slow increments.

Minutes might've passed. Maybe seconds. All he knew was when he lifted his head, Chief Duncan looked at him with compassion and understanding. He didn't want any of that. He didn't want anything but—

"You asked for the day off on Sunday. I was happy that you were finally taking some time for yourself. To have some fun for once. Did something go wrong?"

Well, if he wanted to call having the best sex of his life and falling in love with a woman who made him want to smile all the time wrong, then yeah, something went wrong.

"You never want to talk...about her. Letting the pain out can help. You can be happy. Lynn lost Laura's father at a young age. She still managed to let me love her. It's possible, Aiden. Why are you letting your pain hurt you? Because that's what I think you're doing."

He couldn't deny any of that. He didn't know the complete story behind the death of Laura's father, but he didn't think it could compare to his. Nothing could. Not in his eyes.

"You can ignore me all you want. If it makes you feel better, fine. Don't talk to me." His eyes turned stern. "But stay away from Theresa."

He narrowed his eyes. "And what right do you have to say that to me, Chief? Did she get a restraining order against me? Is that why we're sitting here?"

The chief's eyes shimmered with relief. "No, she didn't." A chuckle escaped. "Finally, I managed to get you to say something. What does that say? You don't like the idea of never seeing her again."

Sighing heavily, he shook his head. "You wouldn't understand."

"Try me." Chief Duncan leaned forward in his chair. "Theresa's a sweet woman. I hate to see her unhappy as I have. I know you're a good guy. I've hated seeing you so unhappy since Cynthia—" He held up his hand to halt any abrupt departure from Aiden, which he thought of doing. "I'm sorry you lost someone you loved dearly. It's never easy. And it's not easy trying it again. I want to help you."

"I..." He hung his head. The words wouldn't come. He couldn't admit what he had done. Not to the chief. Not to anyone.

"You deserve to be happy again, Aiden."

His head shot up. "I don't deserve shit!"

Chief Duncan's brows puckered in confusion. "Why would you say that? You're not walking out of this office without explaining yourself. I'm concerned about you. That comment. That just makes me more worried."

"I…" His breathing became heavy as the words got stuck in his throat again. *Just say it! Spit it out!* His mouth opened and closed several times, yet nothing left. "I…it's my fault."

The pain in his chest receded just a touch. He felt a little lighter voicing those three simple words.

Although, the chief still looked confused. "What is?"

"The…accident." He could do it. "I killed Cynthia."

Done.

He said it.

He finally confessed his horrible crime. And to the chief of police, no less. What the hell had he just done?

Instead of anger and hate and disgust, all he saw on the chief's face was even more confusion. Why wasn't he standing up and demanding he turn around and put his hands behind his back? He killed the woman he was supposed to love. He just confessed.

"Aiden…she died in a car accident. That wasn't your fault."

Leaning toward the desk, he grasped the edge, his fingers digging in hard. "I killed her." Now that he finally admitted to his transgressions, he couldn't stop saying it. Each time he said it, the darkness ebbed away a little more. "I put her in that car and she died."

"It was raining that night. Her car lost control and she hit a tree. So unless you tampered with the car somehow, I still don't know why you believe you killed her."

"She…" His head dropped again, unable to look the

chief in the eyes as he said it. "I broke our engagement that night. I told her I didn't love her anymore and that I wanted to call off the wedding. She left the house upset, crying. She wasn't in the right state of mind to be driving." He lifted his head. "So, yeah, I put her in that car and I killed her."

The chief's expression softened to sympathy. Thank God it wasn't pity because he couldn't bear to see that. "She made the choice to leave that night, did she not?"

He nodded his head in agreement.

"Did you try to stop her?"

He nodded again. "She started throwing stuff. Yelling at me. She ran out of the house and got into her car before I could stop her. I didn't mean to hurt her. I didn't want to hurt her. But I wasn't happy. I was so damn miserable I couldn't take it anymore." He sat back, shoving his hands across his face before dropping them to his lap. "About thirty minutes later, Bentley called me. He arrived first to the scene and saw the car in flames. I guess he panicked. He needed to know if I was in there before he stepped near the vehicle. When you showed up to my house, aware that Bentley called, you saw the mess."

"I did. I just assumed..."

"Yeah, I let you assume I destroyed the house from the news. She did that, Chief, before she stormed out of the house." He let out a heavy sigh. "She could be the sweetest woman in the world, and in the next breath, a raging bitch. I couldn't take her moods anymore. She loved to control my life. I just couldn't take it. I didn't want to feel unhappy anymore. I didn't want to pretend I loved her when I didn't."

"Listen to me closely, Aiden. You did not kill her. She made her own choices that night. You can't keep blaming yourself for something that was out of your control."

"I can't help it."

Chief Duncan smiled. Aiden had no idea how he could even smile after what he confessed.

"It's Thursday. You're only working because O'Connor worked Sunday for you. Not anymore. Take the day off."

"I don't want—"

"Take time to think about everything."

"I hate thinki—"

"Try to let it sink in that you didn't cause her death and that you didn't do anything wrong." The smile on his face grew, as if he didn't hear a damn thing he tried to say. "I heard you volunteered to help with the decorating committee." The laughter in his eyes said he knew exactly what happened there. "So take tomorrow off as well."

"I don't want—"

"I also want you to take the weekend off. I don't want you back to work until Monday."

"But—"

"In fact, I want to see you in my office on Monday before your shift. We'll talk more then."

"Chief, I don—"

"I think you should take this time to enjoy yourself. To let it sink in that you deserve happiness. I think you should start by talking to Theresa. She's miserable. You want to know how I know this? She made a good pot of coffee today. Absolutely delicious. I knew then something was bothering her. She never makes a good pot of coffee."

What could he say to that? Nothing. Because the chief interrupted every time he tried to say something.

"I don't believe you."

Chief Duncan flashed him the brightest smile of the day. "Go see for yourself."

13

AIDEN DECIDED NOT to change out of his uniform before walking to the diner. The entire trek, although it wasn't even a block away from the precinct, felt like a million miles.

He was a jackass. A jerk. Hell, call him a loser.

What kind of man sleeps with a woman and doesn't call her the next day? Well, he figured quite a few might do that. But him? Unforgivable. Especially after the magic they created together.

When he woke up to see her sleeping, so peaceful, so delicate and beautiful, it scared the living daylights out of him. He scrambled out of the bed so fast he was afraid he woke her up. When he realized his jerky movements had done nothing but make her shift a little in her sleep, he hightailed it out of her house so fast he didn't stop to think about what he was doing. When he reached his house, he knew he reacted wrong. His nerves overshadowed his strength to go back there. Or to even call her.

The terror to approach her as he stood outside the diner door was still swamping his veins. He had no idea what to say. Should he just blurt out he loved her? Apologize? Ask her to go out to dinner with him? Perhaps all three would be best. If he even managed to get a simple hello out of his mouth, he'd call it a success.

He knew he didn't deserve her forgiveness. Keeping his distance from her, without calling or visiting her in the diner, was the wrong move. It was insensitive and unworthy of forgiveness, regardless of his reasons.

He yanked the door open and stepped inside. His eyes glided to her immediately at the opposite end of the diner, helping a couple who was most likely passing through town since he didn't recognize them. As a cop, he could identify the residents of Mulberry easily because it was a small town. Almost everyone knew each other.

As he took a seat at the counter to wait for her, not taking his eyes off her, he hated the fact the town was so damn small. That everyone knew everyone and people loved to get in each other's business. He couldn't deny that had been one of the reasons he took so long to break the engagement. He knew the high standard most of the town held him in. He hadn't wanted to disappoint anyone. In the town's eyes, he and Cynthia were the perfect couple. He didn't want to break that illusion and have people look at him with disgust for breaking that perfection.

Now, they just looked at him with pity. Poor Aiden who lost his fiancé so tragically.

If they only knew why she was driving in the pouring rain that night. Because of him. Because of what he had done. Because of what he said.

His words had been hurtful, but truthful. He let all his pain and suffering out that night. The way he disliked her dictating every aspect of their life, even on his daily functions, like taking a damn piss. She hadn't found that funny when he said those exact words. But it was true. That's how he felt. That she even controlled him in such a simple manner.

It was as if she had heard nothing he said. She tried to twist the conversation about her. How the town would look at her. How her father had plans for her and he just needed to follow along. He hadn't realized until that very moment how truly self-absorbed she could be. How selfish.

But he wouldn't say he never loved her. Because he had. He fell in love with the fun-loving, go-getting teenager in high school. All through college, he thought his life was going perfectly and heading for great things with a great woman by his side. As soon as he hurt his knee, it all started to fall apart. Cynthia started to grow a mean streak. She started controlling every little aspect of his life.

The one thing she could never control about him was his job. He loved being a cop. She always tried to get him to work for her father, who worked for the city council. Politics and him. No, thanks.

They should've been married long before her accident. He stretched their engagement out as long as he could, and while she would argue with him, she could never get him to budge. He always found some excuse to prolong picking a wedding date. She should've known from that that he hadn't wanted to commit to her. Hell, he should've known to end it sooner than he had.

A large cup slapped to the counter, sloshing a bit of coffee over the rim and almost on his hand. He looked up to see Theresa's glowing green eyes shimmering with anger and what he could only interpret as pain. So much. All because of him and his jackass behavior.

"Thank you. I—"

"If that's all, I'm really busy today."

He tossed his head both ways, noting how empty the

diner was besides the couple she had been helping when he walked in. "Doesn't look too bad."

"What do you want? Food? An order to go?"

"I want to talk."

Her eyes started to sparkle with what he could only assume as tears starting to form. Shit. He didn't want to see her cry. He stood up. She backed away from the counter, hitting the other counter behind her.

"Please leave. I have nothing to say to you."

"Theresa, I—"

"I'm not a conquest. I'm not a play toy. I'm not a woman that enjoys mind games. Maybe I was asking too much for a simple phone call...but you didn't even come in for your normal cup of coffee. That told me enough. I would like you to leave. I have nothing more to say to you."

He pressed his lips into a hard line, wanting to shout out he loved her. That he was sorry. That he was a world-class jackass. He wouldn't dispute that. But by the tears gathering in strength in the corners of her eyes, he also knew he was a world-class coward. Witnessing her tears would break him.

Grabbing his wallet, he tossed money on the counter, not even glancing how much, and snatched the coffee cup. He turned and started to walk away as he took a sip of coffee. He couldn't hide the wince, although she couldn't see his face, at the horrible taste.

What the hell? Chief Duncan said she made a delicious pot of coffee today. For the first time ever.

You're an idiot. That was his strange way of forcing him to see Theresa. He knew he wouldn't be able to resist to see how great the coffee tasted. If anything, this had to be the worst pot of coffee she'd ever made. Because of him, no doubt.

He pushed open the door and paused, turning toward her. She still stood in the same spot, watching him.

"You're still helping me decorate tomorrow, right?" His heart pounded like mad as he waited for her answer.

"I don't think I'll be able to make it. Goodbye, Officer Crowl."

She effectively just erected the highest, most impenetrable wall she could between them. He hated hearing her call him that.

How did he fix this?

He didn't want to lose her.

———

THERESA FORCED herself to walk away from the fridge. Grabbing the half-empty wine box wouldn't help her. In any way. It didn't take long for her to see her brother standing before her. Or her father. If she took that wine box out, she'd start to turn into them and she couldn't let that happen. She couldn't take the ache in her heart and drown it with alcohol. No. That would just make things worse, not better.

She walked into her dark living room, except for the brightly lit Christmas tree, and slumped down onto the couch.

Seeing his handsome face again today had been torture. Four days. It took him four days to finally come see her.

She didn't know what he wanted to say. An apology, most likely. She didn't want that. She didn't want anything from him anymore.

She had no idea it was possible to fall in love so quickly. If anyone would've asked her a week ago if it were possible, she would've laughed in their faces and said no way. Now, she would say yes.

It was possible.

It happened to her.

And just as quickly, he broke her heart.

Her eyes turned to her tree, trying to soak up some of its happiness into her soul.

Was she overreacting? Was she being too harsh? Maybe his behavior was normal. Did he have to call the next day? Did he have to seek her out? What did she know? She didn't date that often.

But that night...

She couldn't even describe it properly. It had been magical and special, and he ruined that feeling so easily. A simple visit to the diner to grab his usual cup of coffee would've helped to ease her worries. When he never showed up that Monday, as he should've, she knew. That night hadn't meant anything to him. Not like it had to her.

He had the audacity to ask if she would still help decorate tomorrow. After the way he treated her, not going to happen.

The silence that filled the room started to grate on her nerves, but she was too lazy to get up and find her phone. She couldn't even recall where she'd left it. The kitchen, perhaps. Maybe her bedroom. It didn't matter. No one would be calling her. They rarely did.

So she continued to sit in the dark, staring at the Christmas tree, almost dreading the holiday now. She had been looking forward to Christmas day and spending it with Aiden. And now...

Now it'd be a lonely Christmas.

She glanced at her empty coffee table.

Just this morning, she put all of her jewelry supplies away. She completed all of her orders. In record time, too. She hated thinking about Aiden, so to avoid that, she had immersed herself in all the orders she received since Lynn first asked her to make three necklaces.

She made fifteen necklaces. Fifteen!

She still couldn't believe how many people wanted her to make them one. Her idea from the other night didn't seem so farfetched anymore. When she ran it by Bonzo, he agreed. She would now start to display a few pieces of jewelry in the café. People could buy a piece right on the spot, or place an order where they could pick it up at a later date. It was crazy and exhilarating and terrifying all at once. The pleasure of feeling wanted like that, well, she couldn't describe how much it made her want to cry with tears of happiness.

Now if only she could be wanted in an entirely different way.

She stood up. Maybe she'd take a nice hot, relaxing bath. She needed to stop thinking about Aiden.

She grabbed a romance novel she'd been meaning to read for a long time, filled the tub up, and caved in to one glass of wine.

Sliding into the hot tub with her book in one hand and a glass of wine in the other, she sighed.

Was Aiden thinking about her as much as she kept thinking about him?

Probably not.

Well, he asked her if she was still going to help him with the decorations tomorrow. Like a coward, she said no. Honestly, she didn't want to help to begin with. She was never invited to the dumb party.

But it would've been enjoyable to do because she would've been with Aiden. Not anymore. Not after the way he treated her.

She couldn't risk him breaking her heart even more.

So, no. She wouldn't be helping him tomorrow with the decorations.

AIDEN RAISED the bottle to his lips and took a small sip.

A hand slapped his back hard. "Dude, how long have you been here?"

He shrugged as Bentley took a seat next to him at the bar. "An hour or two."

"And how many have you had?"

"Just this one."

Bentley raised a brow as he glanced at the beer bottle in his hand. "You've been here almost two hours and you're still on your first beer? Seriously?" His voice dropped low. "What's going on? You've been weird these last few days."

He fiddled with the label on the bottle, trying to find the right words to explain what the hell was going through his head. Hell, he'd been sitting here for the last two hours trying to sift through the shit going on in his head and he still didn't have a clear picture of what to do.

He felt like he officially lost Theresa. The sad part was he didn't even have her for that long. A day. That's the most he could claim. It made him want to cry. And he didn't even cry when Cynthia died. He was positive some people thought that was odd, especially at the funeral when no tears touched his eyes. He figured most people thought he was in shock. The truth was, shock didn't even begin to cover what he felt that day, or the days after.

"Aiden? Are you okay?"

He caught Bentley's concerned look and glanced away. "I feel like my life is falling apart and I don't know how to fix it."

"Does this have anything to do with Cynthia...or Theresa?"

He lifted the bottle to his lips again and took another small sip, the warm, almost nasty taste of the beer sliding down his throat. "Both, I guess. More so Theresa." He pushed the bottle that he couldn't quite finish away from him. "I screwed up, Bentley. I screwed up big time with her."

"I'm sure you can fix it. Most things with women can be fixed."

"Yeah, you really think so? How'd the problem with you and Daphne turn out?" He looked him in the eye. "Oh, yeah, she's dating another guy."

"Low blow, dude. Very low blow." Bentley sighed. "But so true. I missed my chance with her. So the question is, why are you sitting on your ass, nursing a beer, and missing your chance with Theresa?"

"Because I tried to fix it today and she wouldn't even talk to me."

"Well, if you let her sit too long without doing something else, she probably never will."

Aiden didn't know what to say to that. He glanced down at Stu, the bartender, wondering why he hadn't come to see what drink Bentley wanted. He saw him talking sternly to two people he didn't want to see tonight.

James and Dusty.

"That doesn't look good."

He nodded, agreeing with Bentley's mumbled words. Because it didn't look good. Because the longer he watched Stu talking to them, the more it looked like they wanted to jump across the counter and beat Stu to death.

"Aren't you supposed to be working, filling in a shift for O'Connor?"

"The chief told me not to come in until Monday for work. But it looks like I'm going on duty right now."

Aiden stood up and scooted his stool away as Bentley stared at him strangely, probably wondering why the hell Chief Duncan forced him to take the entire weekend off. He didn't want to get into it. This distraction was perfect to avoid a conversation that he should've never even hinted at. He was hoping for an opportunity to hit Dusty, even James. Dusty for sure, for laying a finger on Theresa. For giving her a bruise.

He could feel Bentley one step behind him as he walked up to the commotion slowly brewing into a full-blown bar fight.

"Problem here, Stu?"

"Well, if ain't Officer Crowl, crime fighting copper of the year." Dusty sneered at him. "Piss off."

"As a matter of fact, Aiden, I was just asking these two gentlemen to leave. They haven't listened yet."

"That's because you have no damn reason to kick us out. We haven't done anything," James spat back.

"Just go somewhere else. Leave peacefully. Home would be the best option. Your sister wants you to stop drinking so much. Why don't you do that for her?"

He knew he should've never said anything, especially mention Theresa. James shoved away from the counter and got right in his face.

"Don't talk to me about my sister. You have no right. Stay the hell away from her."

Aiden flinched at the warning. Did James know he slept with her? Did he know how much he hurt her by ignoring her after the most incredible night ever?

"And why should I do that?" Probably the dumbest thing he could ask, but he had to know.

James' eyes narrowed. "Because I don't like you. I never have. I never will. So do us both a favor and stay the hell away from her."

"Well, do her a favor and stop drinking."

James shoved Aiden hard, knocking him into Bentley. They staggered a bit, but Bentley managed to keep them both upright. He had just enough warning to see the fist coming at him. He jumped out of the way where James ran right into Bentley's fist, going down to the ground without much effort.

Dusty didn't stand back and watch. He charged at Aiden. They obviously drank too much before coming to the bar. It didn't take a great deal of effort for Aiden to dodge both punches thrown by Dusty and take him to the ground. He pulled his arms behind his back and hollered to Stu, "Please tell me O'Connor is almost here. I need some handcuffs."

"Don't worry. I called the police. They should be here soon."

"Get off me, you son of a bitch."

Aiden shoved Dusty harder to the floor, holding his hands tightly together so he couldn't wriggle free. They struggled, Dusty fighting him with everything he had. He wasn't about to receive any help from Bentley as he could hear the grunts as he tussled with James on the floor near the bar.

"Stop fighting me, Dusty. You want more charges added to what's already happening here?"

"I didn't do a damn thing, you asshole."

Aiden couldn't stop the laugh. "Really? How about disorderly conduct for not leaving when Stu asked you to. Assault for trying to hit me." He leaned down, getting close to his ear. "How about the assault the other day. I could tack on that charge, too. Stay the hell away from Theresa. You'll regret it if you don't."

Before Dusty could respond, Chief Duncan was by his side and putting handcuffs on him.

"Thanks, Chief."

Chief Duncan stood up a struggling Dusty and grinned. "I thought I told you to take the day off."

He shrugged and couldn't help but grin back as the chief hauled Dusty out of the bar, O'Connor close behind him with James. Chief Duncan came back in a minute later, after putting Dusty in the back of a patrol car, to get the details of what happened. With Stu's statement, added in with his and Bentley's, it was pretty straight forward what occurred *and* what would happen to James. Another arrest, another opportunity to upset Theresa, and he was partly to blame for it.

Bentley picked up the stools that fell during the scuffle and then patted the counter. "Damn, I need a beer and a shot after that little fiasco."

Taking a spot next to Bentley, Aiden shook his head as Stu pulled out three shot glasses.

"You sure? After dealing with those two, even I need a shot. There was no way in hell I was going to serve them when I knew they were already plastered."

"Trust me, Stu, I'd love to, but I can't now."

Bentley sighed heavily. "You're finally going to get some balls and talk to her."

Stu started to pull one of the shot glasses away. Aiden grabbed it from his hand before it disappeared beneath the bar. "Okay. Maybe one shot. Telling Theresa her brother was arrested again probably won't go so well."

14

SHE PULLED her robe tighter around her as she walked slowly to the door. Only two people would knock this late at night.

Her brother.

Or Aiden.

She wasn't sure which one she preferred. Her drunk ass brother that could potentially turn into a phone call to the police. That didn't sound like fun to deal with.

Or Aiden, where he would...what? Try to weasel his way back into her bed, then leave without a word goodbye and ignore her for four days straight?

She took a deep breath before peering through the peephole. Without turning on the porch light, which she had no intention of doing, it made it difficult to see. Although, she saw her answer clear enough.

Aiden was the winner.

Should she open the door?

When he knocked again, a little harder this time, she knew he wouldn't leave until she did. With great reluctance, although she needed to deal with him eventually, she unlocked the door and pulled it open.

His eyes flashed with desire as soon as she made eye contact. Yeah, well, he wasn't getting back in her bed again. Not after last time.

"What do you want, Officer Crowl? It's late."

He clenched his jaw. "I told you to call me Aiden." His features softened. "Can I come in please? It's freezing out and we need to talk."

"I have nothing to say to you."

"It's about your brother. So let me in."

Her brother? What had he done now? She glanced at his clothes and noticed he wasn't in his uniform. Had something bad happened to him?

"Is he alright? What happen—"

Aiden stepped closer and placed a calm hand on her shoulder. "He's fine." His features turned fierce. "He was arrested. Bar fight...one where he pushed me, then took a swing at Bentley."

"Why would he..." She backed up. His hand fell away. While that's why she backed away, she missed his touch. "He was drunk, wasn't he?"

Aiden nodded.

"You didn't need to come tell me this."

"It wasn't my only reason for coming, although I did prefer to tell you since it partly involved me. I'm sorry he had to get arrested again."

"Are you? Are you really that sorry?"

"Yes, damn it. I know he's your brother and you care about him. It hurts you when he does this. I even tried to tell him that and..." His gaze turned down.

"And what?"

He lifted his eyes back to her. "He told me to stay away

from you. And that's exactly what I did all week and it was the hardest thing I ever did." He took a step closer, almost standing in her doorway. "It was the dumbest thing I ever did. Please forgive me, Theresa. I told you I wouldn't be good at this relationship stuff. Give me another chance."

Even in the cold, dark night, she could see the pain in his eyes. The truth. He meant what he said. She didn't doubt that. But what she had a hard time understanding was how he couldn't be good at the relationship stuff, as he put it. He excelled at it with Cynthia. Why did he find it so difficult with her?

Because he couldn't possibly ever fall in love with her like he had with Cynthia. That could be the only explanation. And it wasn't one she liked. It wasn't one she wanted to compete with. Her heart would never survive.

"Theresa? Say something. Anything. Let me come inside and we can talk about this. About us."

Us.

There would never be an us. She knew this from the beginning, but like an idiot, she thought it could turn out differently. She knew better now.

As lightly as possible, soaking up the way her hand touched his hard chest, she pushed him back outside onto the porch stoop. "There is no us. I don't think this is going to work. If we're both being honest, I don't think it was ever going to work. We're two different people from two different worlds." She moved back, gripping the door hard. "Thank you for telling me about my brother. I appreciate that. Have a good night, Officer Crowl."

With that, she shut the door before he could say another word.

And yes, she addressed him by his formal title, as she would from now on. She needed to maintain a distance with him, and she couldn't do that if she continued to call him Aiden.

She quickly locked the door and ran to her room, almost as if he were inside and chasing her. Flinging herself across the bed, she buried her head into the soft contours of the bedspread.

Had she done the right thing? Should she have let him in to talk? What could he have possibly said to make things better?

Nothing.

Nothing could make things better between them.

They were doomed from the very beginning. She had done the right thing.

So why did it feel so wrong?

AIDEN STOOD off to the side, trying not to think about Theresa and listen to the instructions given by Donna Contreas, the event organizer for the annual Christmas party for Mulberry.

Bentley stood next to him, munching on a cookie provided by Lynn. He loved her delicious treats she baked all the time, but he wasn't in the mood. Shit. He wasn't in the mood for anything, especially decorating for this party.

Not after Theresa effectively cut him out of her life. She didn't even want to hear his explanation, well it was more of an apology. He didn't blame her. Not really. He acted like a jackass and he didn't deserve another chance. It still hurt. The loss of her.

"You should try a grin."

He jabbed Bentley in the side. "Shut up."

"You're bringing the mood down."

Glancing around the room at everyone present to help decorate, he saw Marybeth, Gregory—Chief Duncan's dad —as well his girlfriend Gabby, a few of the council members, and Daphne.

"Why are you here again?" He snickered under his breath. "Oh, yeah, to catch a glimpse of Daphne."

"Are you trying to get me to match your sullen mood?"

"If you don't shut up and leave me alone, yeah."

"Point taken."

Thankfully, Bentley shut up and they both listened with half an ear on how Donna wanted everything placed. Seemed simple enough. Hang the lights and make them look pretty. Set up tables and chairs. Hang shit on the wall. The basic decorations for any holiday party.

The Christmas tree, which was most likely the hardest thing to situate, already stood tall and proud in the middle of the ballroom. Bright white lights twinkled around it as white glittery balls hung here and there. He had to admit it looked beautiful. Of course, it didn't look as beautiful as the tree he and Theresa decorated, but he figured most people would ooh and aah over it.

"You coming to the party tomorrow?"

"No."

Bentley laughed. "How long are you going to sulk over Theresa?"

"How long have you been sulking over Daphne?"

A low groan left his mouth. "It is so difficult to make you see anything when you keep throwing that shit in my face."

He turned to Bentley and grinned. It felt sort of good to grin when his entire life felt like shit. "Then quit trying to make me see anything. Because it can all apply to you, too, buddy."

"I know. That's why I hate it when you do that." Bentley smirked. "At least you have a small chance."

"Yeah, I'm pretty sure I have zero chances."

"You sure about that?" Bentley nudged his shoulder with his own. "Because a gorgeous woman just walked into the room."

Aiden followed Bentley's line of sight to the entrance of the ballroom and nearly dropped to his knees. Standing somewhat awkwardly and perhaps even nervously was Theresa. What was she nervous about? She was utterly perfect in every way.

"Why are you still standing by me? Go walk up to her."

With a slight push on the back from Bentley, he made his way over to Theresa, Donna's voice effectively drowned out completely. He didn't understand the need for such long instructions anyway. Just hang the decorations and be done. Pretty simple.

His eyes locked with Theresa's. Could she feel the same magical pull as him? Was that why her eyes didn't move from his?

"I didn't think I'd see you here."

Wringing her hands together, she glanced down, then back up. "Bonzo said I could leave a little early. I said I'd help. I should've never said I couldn't make it. I'm not someone who backs out of a responsibility just because..." Her eyes glanced down again. "Where do we start?"

He knew she was talking about putting up Christmas stuff, but he wanted to answer so differently. He wanted to start over. Wipe the slate clean. He wanted to pull her into his arms and kiss her.

"Donna hasn't gotten to that part yet. She's been talking about how to hang things for the past fifteen minutes. I almost took a nap."

The corner of her lips tilted up. Score one for him. He almost made her smile. And damn, he loved it when she smiled.

"I'm glad you're here."

Just like that, her near smile turned into a frown. "I'm not here for you. I'm here because I told Marybeth I'd help." Her brows puckered. "She never did give you any instructions, did she?"

He tried to grin just a little, hoping to pull another smile out of her. "I don't think she ever had any. It was just a ploy to—" His pathetic grin evaporated as her face turned even more melancholy. He took a step closer. "Can we start over? I would love that. I know I don't deserve another chance after the way I acted, but...please, Theresa. Just one more chance."

Her mouth opened, yet nothing came out. He wanted so badly to urge her on. To make her say the words he wanted to hear.

"I don—"

"Let's do this!" Donna clapped loudly, a wide smile on her face, effectively cutting off Theresa's response.

He couldn't even be mad at her for finally finishing her long speech of instructions and interrupting Theresa because he didn't think what Theresa was about to say would've been in his favor.

Within seconds, she disappeared and went to help Gabby, who started to hang lights around the doorframe that led to a separate hallway with more rooms and the bathrooms.

He knew another chance to win her back was officially over. He joined Bentley and started to unfold tables and chairs and set them up around the room. They made a wide arc around the room, setting up the tables that would be used for food and drinks. The chairs were situated against the walls for people to sit in if they needed a moment of rest. The remaining area would be kept clear for people to mingle and to dance if the need came over them.

He couldn't recall anyone ever actually dancing at one of these parties, because Christmas music was played in the background, but he almost wished for a moment Theresa would go with him and dance with him. He wanted her back in his arms.

But what was he thinking? She didn't even want to come to this party. Hell, he didn't either. He only went every year for Cynthia, because she insisted they go.

A few hours later, after unfolding so many tables and chairs and hanging lights all around the room, he was tired. He wanted to go home and just be alone. Maybe wallow in some self-pity. Think of a great way to win Theresa's heart back. He wasn't ready to give up. He finally knew what he wanted in life, what made him truly happy. He wasn't ready to give up because she was throwing off I-hate-you vibes. He hadn't almost made it as a pro football player because he gave up so easily. If he never would've hurt his knee as badly as he had, he'd probably be rich and famous and playing ball like he used to love doing.

He didn't want money or fame. It was the love for the game he missed.

His hands dropped after hanging what he hoped to be the last decoration and he sighed. Well, hell. That's why Cynthia had always been on his case to work for her father. That's why she changed from a sweet girl to a hellion. Because he missed his chances of going pro. Missed his chance at fame and fortune. Cynthia never understood him and the dreams he wanted.

She always liked being in the limelight, the attention

focused solely on her. Being with a pro football player would've upped her status. Then in a blink of an eye, he was a cop. Nothing fancy about that.

He made the right decision. Even though she died tragically, and he still felt responsible for that, he made the best decision he could have. They weren't meant for each other. She used him, and he didn't want to be with a woman who acted that way. He wanted someone who would love him for the man he was, not the man they wanted him to be. To appreciate what was inside him, not what he could offer on the outside.

Theresa was that woman.

"Shit." How would he make it right between them?

A light tap to his shoulder startled him, making him twist around quickly. The movement almost had Theresa falling over as his arm swung and hit her in the stomach. He immediately grabbed her around the waist and pulled her gently into his arms.

"I'm so sorry. Did I hurt you?"

Her mouth hung open, her eyes wide with shock.

"Theresa?"

"No. No. I'm fine. I didn't mean to startle you." She calmly pushed against his chest and he let his arms drop at once. He didn't want to make her uncomfortable, even though it felt wonderful to have her in his arms again.

"I was thinking..." Yeah, he didn't know if he should tell her he was thinking about her. Honestly, he had no idea what to say to her. "Thanks for coming tonight."

She nodded and wrapped her arms around her stomach, as if trying to ward him off. "I just wanted to say...I don't want there to be any hard feelings between us. It's a small town and...I don't want it to be awkward." She let out a tiny breath. "Can we still be friends?"

Oh, man. She was breaking his heart. Friends? He didn't want to be just friends with her. But he screwed up. Instead of pulling her closer after the most amazing night ever, he pushed her away. Maybe to work his way into her good graces, he'd have to take what she offered now. Friends only.

"Okay."

"Okay?"

She sounded way too surprised at his response. Should he have argued? Should he have demanded he wanted more? Was that what she wanted him to do? Was that what he should do? God, he was so lost.

He blew out a heavy breath as his eyes twisted upward in frustration. Trying to win back the heart of the woman he loved was more than just difficult, it was tragically impossible. He lowered his gaze back to her, and confusion, hurt, anger, even desire, all shimmered within her depths. She was just as lost as him.

Without taking time to think of how she'd respond, he grabbed her arm and pulled her gently to him, pressing his lips to hers. His arms slid around her, molding her to his body as he urged her mouth to open. She didn't resist, brushing her tongue with his.

The kiss felt perfect, and like he finally found his true home.

But she wanted to be only friends. He had to work with what he had at the moment, and shoving his hunger for her in her face in a public place wasn't the right thing to do. He knew that.

Reluctantly, he broke the kiss and let his hands fall away from her.

"What are you doing?" she asked breathlessly.

He pointed above them to the mistletoe he had hung right before she tapped him on the shoulder. "Mistletoe. You have to kiss when you're under one. Even if we're only friends."

She glanced up, then dropped her gaze to his. "Oh. Well, I guess I'll be going."

"It's late. Let me give you a ride home. I don't want you walking by yourself in the dark." In fact, the thought frightened him. Not that Mulberry was a dangerous town, but still. A woman, a beautiful woman, walking home in the dark by herself had trouble written all over it.

"It's nice of you to offer, but Gregory and Gabby already said they'd drop me off. Goodbye, Off—"

"It's Aiden." His jaw clenched tightly to stop himself from saying something he'd regret. "You want to be friends, then you call me Aiden."

She nodded once, then walked away.

As he stood under the mistletoe that put the woman who captured his heart back in his arms, he wondered where to go from here. She wanted to be friends still. She didn't seem to hate him anymore. But she also hadn't forgiven him if she wanted to maintain a friends-only kind of relationship.

His eyes glided to the mistletoe above him.

Perhaps it was time for a big grand gesture to show her he truly loved her.

15

———

THERESA SLOUCHED into her couch trying not to feel sorry for herself. After much internal arguing, she gave in to help decorate. She wasn't a person who said she'd do something and then not actually do it. She knew seeing Aiden would be difficult, but she refused to look like an untrustworthy person. The minute he asked her to help decorate and she accepted, the entire town knew. And if she didn't show up, they'd also know that.

It wasn't so bad last night. She helped Gabby the entire night, while Aiden worked closely with Bentley. She couldn't help but toss glances his way here and there. Sometimes, their eyes connected. Other times, she soaked up everything she could before he turned her way.

Stringing lights and helping to display the holiday spirit gave her time to think, gave her perspective on their situation. The holidays should bring forth happiness, not sorrow and pain. That's exactly what she was doing to herself, and she didn't like feeling that way.

So what he hadn't called her the next day. So what he hadn't shown up for his normal cup of coffee. It's not like he had to do those things. They had sex, and that's it. She just wanted to move on. But she also didn't want any weird tension between them. That's why she put the truce out there and asked if they could still be friends.

And he agreed.

Her heart broke a little more when he had. Silly her. She wanted him to profess his love and pull her into his arms and kiss her.

Well, he had done the latter. He just hadn't done the first thing. Profess his love.

He probably never would, and she needed to accept that.

She had never written a bucket list before, although at times thought of a few things she'd add if she ever wrote one. She could cross one item off.

~~Sleep with Aiden Crowl~~.

She could now put her ridiculous crush behind her.

The other thing on her imaginary bucket list would be to get her brother some help.

She tried to refrain as long as she could. She had really, really tried. But she couldn't do it. On her lunch break yesterday, she swung by the jail to pay his bail. To her complete surprise, someone else had already paid it. When she asked with the sweetest smile she possessed who had, the officer behind the desk refused to tell her.

Who would pay his bail? She always did. Of course, he wasn't arrested that often, but the few times he got locked up, she was there for him. Her mother never had any money to do it, and her father, who knew where he was?

She tried to call James, but he didn't answer. Ignoring her like he enjoyed doing lately. There was no way she'd visit him at Dusty's house again, so she let it go.

The problem with letting it go was he needed to get help. Because one of these days she would lose her brother entirely, the good man she knew he could be. He was hidden somewhere inside that persona he showed off to the world.

By the time she got back to the diner, her mood was terrible, especially when she couldn't get rid of the concern about who might've bailed her brother out and why he wouldn't answer her phone call. It didn't take Bonzo long to increase her mood to disastrous levels when he reminded her about the Christmas decorating. Not that she forgot about it, because it had been on her mind the entire morning, making her sick to her stomach that she told him she wouldn't be there.

But she had gone and he kissed her and touched her and it all made her wish for things she couldn't have.

Her eyes glided to her Christmas tree all lit up in its beautiful glory. That happy holiday spirit she had hoped to regain from making amends with Aiden still wasn't there. Even staring at her lovely tree.

All day, being a Saturday where she didn't have to work, she had done nothing but pine and think and wonder what Aiden was doing. Here, late into the evening, she still couldn't help but do the same thing.

Was she wrong in offering friends only? Maybe they should just ignore each other. Maybe it would be easier on her heart. He agreed way too quickly for her tastes. Hell, she wished he never agreed at all.

Why couldn't he love her? Would she ever find a man who loved her as much as he loved Cynthia?

"You're being pathetic right now, Theresa."

Standing up, she blew out a large breath and stomped out of the dark living room to the kitchen.

She had done the right thing. Nothing would ever work out between her and Aiden. Being friends would have to be okay. He agreed, so she just had to believe she made the right decision.

As best as she could, she had to avoid mistletoes when he was near. Because apparently, even as friends, they would kiss.

Maybe that wasn't such a bad thing. Maybe she could seduce him—

No. She wasn't that kind of woman. She didn't seduce men. If he couldn't love her on his own, she wouldn't force the issue.

Grabbing a bag of pretzels to binge on, she walked to her bedroom and situated herself onto the bed. Eating her troubles away couldn't be a bad thing if she ate something somewhat healthy. Within a few minutes, her mind tried to center on her romance novel as she nibbled on pretzels.

She would stop thinking about Aiden. Nothing good would come from thinking about him anyway. He was working. It's not like he was thinking about her.

———

"I AM SO glad that shit is done. Don't ever ask me to help you again."

Aiden chuckled as he walked Bentley to the door. "I hope I never screw up this badly again to ask for your help." The smile on his face dimmed. "If this even works."

Bentley's hand stalled on the door handle. "It will. She'll love it. Just don't ask me to do something like this ever again. It just ain't right." He chuckled.

"Maybe you should make a big grand gesture to Daphne. Show her what man she should be with. Fair is fair. I'll help you."

Bentley's lips twisted in frustration and angst. "I think I

should start to move on from thinking about her anymore. If she's happy, then I'm happy for her." His brows dipped low. "I just don't get her boyfriend. If it was me, I would've had a ring on her finger already. Two years, man. Way too long."

Aiden hated when Bentley said that, because it made him think of Cynthia and how long he waited—for everything.

"Maybe he doesn't want to marry her. Maybe there's a reason he hasn't asked."

"She's amazing. Why wouldn't he want to marry her? He's an idiot. Any man who waits that long is one."

It was as if Bentley punched him hard in the face. He couldn't dispute the words. He *was* an idiot. He should've ended his relationship with Cynthia long before it got as far as it had.

"I waited...a long time. In fact, I didn't even ask Cynthia. She just said we were getting married and that was that."

Bentley's hand dropped from the door. "Yeah, she had a way about her sometimes."

"She...uh..."

Although Bentley was his best friend, he didn't always share every little thing with him. Especially about Cynthia. He didn't want to appear like a wimp, or a loser, or someone who was controlled easily, even though he felt like all three of those things when he was with her.

A sigh escaped as Bentley shrugged. "Cynthia was..."

"Controlling. I let her control me. I let her plan my life when it wasn't something I wanted. I never asked her to marry me because I didn't want to marry her. I never let her set a wedding date because I dreaded marrying her. I...I broke our engagement the night of her accident. That's why..."

A hand grasped his shoulder in a comforting embrace. A

signal of understanding. "That's why you've struggled so much with her death. I had a feeling you weren't happy with her. Then...you seemed so torn up, I figured I imagined it. It's because you feel guilty, isn't it?"

"She would've never been driving that night if we hadn't been fighting. You know her when she got in a mood. She was hysterical and crying and she just rushed out of the house..." He shook his head in agony as he lowered his gaze to the floor. It was so difficult to say. But strangely, he felt lighter each time he said it, which made it a little easier every time he opened his mouth. He might have to thank Chief Duncan for making him talk, because the more he talked about it, the lighter he felt inside. The darkness was slowly ebbing away.

"That shit isn't your fault, man. She made her own choices." Bentley squeezed his shoulder hard to get his point across. "And now you found a woman that makes you happy. I know she does because I can see my friend coming back from the dead. For a while there, I didn't think I'd ever see the real you again. I'm almost tempted to buy Theresa the best Christmas present ever for giving me back my best friend."

His head shot up. "I have been horrible. But no more. I promise. I still feel responsible for her death, but—"

"Don't." Bentley shook his head. "Don't let her control you even in death, man. That's what's happening. Just let it all go. Focus on Theresa. Focus on you, for once."

No truer words were ever spoken. He even tried to tell himself not to let Cynthia control him beyond the grave. It wasn't something he could just stop at a moment's notice. It'd take time. But time wasn't on his side right now. He needed to shove those thoughts away. Far away. He needed to win Theresa's heart. His plan had to work.

"I'd ask if you want to hang out tomorrow since we both have off, but...I hope your plan for Theresa works."

"Me, too. Wish me luck."

Bentley glanced down the hallway to everything they set up and smiled. "I don't think you're going to need any luck. Who knew you were such a romantic? I guess only Theresa knows how to pull that out of you."

So much truth in those words. He had never shown any romantic gestures with Cynthia. Ever. Everything he had done today, everything he planned to do, was new to him. So he hoped he was doing the right thing. What the hell did he, or even Bentley, know about romance?

"Are you going to call her tonight?"

Aiden pulled his phone out of his pocket and cringed. "It's kind of late. She might not appreciate me knocking on her door at ten o'clock. What do you think?"

"Wait until tomorrow. Plan a whole day for her. Women like sweet shit like that."

Bentley turned toward the door, opened it, then paused in the doorway when his phone beeped a loud siren.

"What the hell is that?"

"A text message from the station. That only goes off when there's a big fire to handle." Bentley pulled his phone out of his pocket, swiping a finger across the screen. The frown that pierced his lips concerned Aiden.

"Do they need you? Where's the fire at?"

Bentley's eyes turned from the phone to him, an air of panic written in the depths. "Shit, man. I think it's Theresa's house."

16

LARGE ORANGE FLAMES SPARKED across the dark night. The entire drive he sat in the passenger seat of Bentley's truck, stoic and quiet. He lost one woman to anger and pain, and now he was losing another.

The fire chief didn't report much in the text besides a location and the status of the fire. By the way Bentley started running for his truck, he knew the status was bad. He was one step behind him, slamming his way in the passenger side. He didn't even stop to grab a jacket from the closet.

Bentley knew better than to speak. And really, what could he say? Theresa's house was in flames. Why? Was she okay?

They saw the first flash of orange a mile away. It tore through his gut, ripping it to shreds within seconds. Eyeing that from such a distance told him one thing—the entire house was engulfed in flames. Had she made it out safely?

The truck jerked to a hard stop behind a row of patrol vehicles and fire trucks down Theresa's lane. It was a narrow street, her house the last one. So far the fire hadn't jumped to the neighboring houses. Perhaps the snow and cold weather could be thanked for that. He had no clue. He just needed to know Theresa made it out safely.

Suddenly, his emotions sprang loose. All his horror and terror hearing those few words broke free like a wild lion running rampant through a zoo beyond its cage. He pushed the truck door open hard and started running toward the heavy flames dancing in the night sky.

He didn't stop to think about what he was doing. He didn't question the stupidity of running into a burning building. His legs just stretched as far as they could with each step that took him closer to the house that held the woman he loved.

Without warning, a large body tackled him from behind, slamming them both brutally to the ground. The cold, wet pavement barely registered as he struggled with the heavy body on top of him. He didn't even care who knocked him down. His only thought was to save the woman he loved. He needed Theresa in his life like he needed to take his next breath. She was vital to his survival. He'd never recover if he lost her, especially like this.

"Get off me!"

"Calm the hell down, Aiden!"

He should've known. Bentley had his arms wrapped tightly around his middle, holding him face down to the ground. They both played on the high school football team. While he had been the quarterback, Bentley had played the linebacker position. They had both been stars on the team.

"Let me go. I need to get in there."

Bentley's voice was low and measured. "No one's going in there. It's not safe. The fire...it's everywhere, man. Let's ask if she got out before you go crazy. Calm down. Please."

He was about to fight for his life, jabbing an elbow, kicking a leg, hell, get a bite in somewhere to break free of the hold Bentley had on him when a stern yet even voice said, "She's safe. Let him up, Bentley."

The arms around him disappeared. He turned slightly to see Chief Duncan standing before him with a hand outstretched. He took his hand without complaint, letting him help him up. Chief Duncan didn't release Aiden's hand when he stood to his full height, almost tightening his grip as he pulled him a bit closer.

"She's shaken up. She has some smoke inhalation, a cut on her arm, but otherwise she's fine. They took her to the hospital." He tried to break the grip, but Chief Duncan increased the pressure even more, refusing to let go. "I'll drive you myself. But Bentley's right. Calm down. She's okay."

"I'm calm."

Chief Duncan grinned. "Now you are. You almost ran right into a burning building without thinking. Don't make me do something I'd hate to do."

He didn't even want to know what that meant, so instead of asking, he nodded that he would stay calm. At least, he hoped so. As soon as he could see Theresa's face for himself that she was safe, he could relax. The longer that took, well, he couldn't guarantee anything.

Glancing around, he realized Bentley had rushed to one of the fire trucks, putting his gear on to help extinguish the beast blazing before them.

Chief Duncan loosened his grip, then let his hand go, slapping a hand to his shoulder to move him along. "Let's go. I know you want to see her."

"Did you see her?"

"No. The fire chief relayed the news to me because it was the first thing I asked when I arrived."

"Then how do you know she's okay? She could be—"

The hand on his shoulder increased in strength. "I said to stay calm. Take slow, deep breaths if you have to. The fire chief said she's okay. If he said that, I believe him."

Yeah, well, he didn't hold that same belief. He'd only believe it with his own eyes. He needed to see her right this instant.

The drive to the hospital was the longest drive of his life. Almost longer than the drive to her house. He noticed the chief was dressed up nicely in a suit. He must've dashed out of the Christmas party when he heard the news about the fire, which he figured the news spread very quickly. The fire was so big, they probably saw it from the hotel, the flames dancing in the dark sky.

The minute the chief pulled into a spot in the emergency room parking lot, Aiden dashed out of the car. The voice echoing in the distance to stay calm didn't slow him down as he charged through the door and to the front desk. He nearly sent a stack of papers sitting on the ledge to the floor.

Erin, the nurse by the desk, had quick hands as she grabbed them before they tumbled to the floor.

"Officer Crowl? Are you—"

"Where is she? Theresa Brennen. I need to see her. Where is she?"

Erin took a step back, probably because he shouted the words at her instead of just asking in a nice, relaxed voice.

"She's in—"

"He doesn't need to know yet."

His eyes narrowed at Chief Duncan. "You have no right."

"You're losing it, Aiden. Do you hear yourself? Do you know how you just spoke to Erin? You can't go into her room until you calm down. You're going to scare her. Right now, Theresa doesn't need that."

Shit. The chief was right, of course. He just didn't know how to stop the raging energy coursing through his veins. All he knew was he needed to see her face. He needed to see she was okay. He knew with one look into her eyes he would calm down.

The angry twist of his face didn't scare the chief into giving in. It did nothing but increase his rage at the delay. He needed to see her. Now. He was getting so upset he was ready to charge at the chief and take him to the ground for keeping him away from Theresa.

He figured the chief knew it, too, as he braced his feet wider apart, getting ready for the hit. His eyes caught the slight movement in the chief's hands. A nervous twitch.

Suddenly, he bent and shoved his head between his legs, trying to breathe in and out in a steady, calm manner. It was hard as hell.

What was he doing? Why was he acting like a maniac? He knew this wasn't easy for the chief. It's not as if Chief Duncan spoke about it, but he saw the torture he went through when his mother had cancer. The dread that would cross his face to visit her again in the hospital, yet he had done it faithfully every day until the day she succumbed to the terrible disease. The chief hated the hospital. Yet, here he stood with him, offering him comfort and preventing him from scaring the hell out of Theresa. Which he would if he walked into her room like a half-raged banshee.

It took a few seconds, or maybe it was minutes, to control his breathing. Slow, deep breaths released, helping him to find the composure he lacked since learning about the fire.

He stood back up and blew out another deep breath. His gaze went to Erin first. "I apologize for my behavior. It was inexcusable."

She smiled lightly. "It's not easy when someone you care about is injured. I understand. Are you ready?" Although she asked him the question, her eyes darted to Chief Duncan when she asked it.

"Do you want me to walk with you?"

Aiden declined the chief's offer. He just wanted to hold Theresa in his arms, no prying eyes on them.

Well, if she even let him do that. What kind of reception would he receive? It didn't matter. He didn't think he'd be able to keep his hands to himself.

When he walked into the room and saw Theresa sitting up in bed, a large white bandage across her forearm, he nearly lost it and the composure he worked so hard to restore out in the lobby of the hospital.

Tears filled her eyes at the sight of him. He didn't stop to think, to hesitate, to do anything but make the few steps it took to get to her side and pull her into his arms. She accepted him with ease and sank her head to his chest. Light tears sprinkled onto his shirt right away.

She was safe. His eyes finally confirmed it, which meant his heart could slow down. Yet it didn't. Because he had so much to say. So much he needed to tell her. He decided to start with the most important thing.

"I love you, Theresa." His embrace tightened. "I love you so damn much."

THE TEARS BECAME HEAVIER at his admission. He loved her. She couldn't believe it. Maybe she misheard.

The sound of his soft voice repeating his whispered words of love confirmed how much he loved her, that she wasn't mishearing a thing. He couldn't seem to stop saying it. She wasn't about to impede his speech of love, which honestly just consisted of him saying *I love you* over and over. It was enough for her. It's as if a miracle had occurred. She never thought she'd hear those three little words from him.

Would he still love her when she told him who started the fire? Would that love survive her confession?

She needed to get herself together. She needed to tell him and then watch him walk out of the room with disgust. He would. *She* wanted to walk out, because she loathed herself.

Her tears stopped as the icky feeling in her stomach overwhelmed any other emotion trying to escape. Even after her eyes dried of tears, he still didn't let go of her. Instead of fighting him, she just soaked up his warm embrace, imagining she wouldn't have it as soon as they started to talk.

Then, to her dismay, he lowered his arms in a smooth stroke down her back and pulled away, cupping her chin. A light kiss brushed across her lips. She savored every little touch he was willing to give her.

"Are you okay?"

She nodded, afraid to speak. Afraid everything would come tumbling out and then her world would crumble.

"I nearly...I almost..." He kissed her lips again, harder this time.

She opened to him, letting him soothe her rattled nerves with the flick of his tongue against hers. The anxiety threatening to climb out of her skin slowly dimmed as his sweet, strong kiss pushed it away.

Breaking the kiss, he rested his forehead against hers. "I don't know anything. How did you get out? Talk to me."

Like that, the stress level skyrocketed to the roof. She couldn't have his arms around her as she told him. She wouldn't be able to bear the pain when he eventually shoved her away in revulsion. So she did it first, pushing him away.

He looked confused, but stood up from the bed. He didn't back away, though.

"It's okay. We don't have to talk about anything right now. Do you need to stay for observation? The chief said something about smoke inhalation. At least tell me that."

He looked so pained about everything it made her heart hurt with so much agony.

"I didn't inhale much. My throat doesn't hurt or anything." She didn't want to talk about it, but delaying the inevitable never worked out. It would be better if she got the worst part over with. "I decided to get ready for bed. I opened my bedroom door to go to the kitchen for some water and all this smoke just hit my face. I thought about running through it to get outside, but then I saw the fire at the edge of the hallway. I had to break my bedroom window and climb out that way because I couldn't get the lock to budge. I cut my arm on the way out." She lifted her arm with the bandage wrapped around it.

He jerked as if he wanted to sit down, then changed his mind. "I'm glad you got out safely. You're lucky you didn't fall asleep. I wonder what the hell started the fire."

That's where he was going to start hating her. Because she started the fire. She burned her house down. She almost killed herself because of her stupidity.

At least she knew he loved her for a moment. She would treasure that for the rest of her life.

"I started the fire. It was my fault." Her confession didn't make her feel lighter. If anything, it weighed her down even further.

His frown was fierce as his brows puckered low. "I don't understand. Why?"

"It was an accident." Perhaps he wouldn't hate her as much if he believed that. "I forgot to unplug my Christmas tree. I forget all the time. Because I'm an idiot, a fire started."

No one would be able to make her think otherwise.

"You're an idiot alright, but you didn't start the fire."

They both jerked their attention to the doorway. James stood tall and furious.

17

"WHAT THE HELL are you doing here?" Aiden couldn't have stopped the angry retort if he had tried.

"Gee, I don't know. My sister barely escaped a fire and died."

"You know what I mean." His eyes narrowed as he stared hard at James. He didn't flinch or break the stare with him.

"I'm okay." Theresa's whispered words broke some of the tension swimming between them.

James walked to the other side of the bed and grabbed his sister's hand. "Are you? Because I nearly had a heart attack when I heard what was happening. I might have more charges slapped on me, too, because I hit the security guard and left."

Her brows fell into confusion. "What are you talking about? I tried calling you. Where have you been?"

Aiden's eyes connected with James', but he decided to let her brother handle how he wanted to explain everything.

"You know I'm not a fan of this jackass. He's an asshole, and you should stay away from him."

Well, he didn't like to hear *that.* Would Theresa listen to him? She loved her brother. Even when he acted like a drunken idiot, she loved him. But he had professed his love. Repeatedly, in fact. Not once did she repeat the words back. Maybe what he felt for her was all one-sided. Maybe she didn't love him. Whatever she said to James' words would tell him how she felt towards him.

"I know that already. What does that have to do with where you were?"

"What, the golden boy didn't tell you what he did?"

She glanced between him and James, the confusion even brighter. He didn't say a word. He didn't do what he did to get into her good graces. Well, maybe a little. He did it because he knew it would make her happy. After the way he made her sad, that's all he wanted. To make her happy again.

"Just tell me, James."

"He paid my bail, even though he's the reason I got locked up to begin with."

"Sure. I pushed you and caused a scene in the bar while I was drunk off my ass." Never again would he help this asshole. Then his eyes connected with Theresa and he knew that was a lie. Of course he'd help James again just to make her smile.

"You paid my brother's bail? Why?"

"Yeah, *Officer Crowl*, why?" James asked in a mocking tone.

Sitting on the bed, ignoring the painful fact she pushed him away a few minutes ago, he grabbed her hand that her brother wasn't holding. "James is forgetting one important fact. There was one condition for me to pay his bail—he had to get help. He agreed to enter a treatment facility. The one near Mason. You know the one I'm talking about." She nodded. "He isn't supposed to have contact with anyone for thirty days and he wasn't supposed to leave." He turned his head to glare at James.

"Fire. My sister. Do the damn math, *Officer Crowl*."

"Quit calling me that, especially in that tone of voice."

"Please stop arguing." Her quiet voice was his undoing.

He bent closer, almost touching her lips, despite that her brother stood in the room. "I love you. I will do everything in my power to always make you happy, even if I don't like doing it."

She closed the distance and pressed her lips to his. The kiss was brief but enough to satisfy him. It told him more than any words could express.

He backed away and looked at James. "What did you mean when you walked in? Do you think someone deliberately started the fire?"

James let go of Theresa's hand and started to pace next to the bed. "Yeah, I do, and I almost didn't come to the hospital. I want to kill him."

"Him, who?" He needed James to get to the point. He wasn't above beating the answer out of him. He didn't like the thought that someone would deliberately hurt Theresa. It made no sense. She was so damn sweet.

James stopped pacing. The sorrow and regret on his face almost had him bending his feelings to like the guy just a little. Not a lot, because he didn't think he would ever like James, but just a touch.

"Dusty."

Theresa gasped. Her hand trembled within his. He squeezed lightly to calm her down and offer some comfort. A little for himself, if he was being honest.

"Did he touch you?" James almost loomed over her. He must've seen the warning flash in Aiden's eyes because he backed up a step. "He started spouting his mouth off after we got locked up. He's damn lucky he was in the cell next to mine and not sharing one because I would've started beating the living shit out of him. Did he touch you?"

Theresa frowned. "He didn't hurt me."

Aiden couldn't hold in the snort. "You fell and bruised your cheek because of him. He obviously didn't—"

Well, shit. Had his words to Dusty, his warning, make him retaliate against Theresa?

He looked at James. "What makes you think he started the fire? What did he say to you?"

The fierce look on James' face said he wanted to know more about the bruise. "He said Theresa was a tease. When I asked him to clarify, he wouldn't. Then he said some shit about you and called her a tease again." He rubbed a hand over his jaw. "I have no proof he started the fire, but when I heard there was a fire in town and the address, I just knew he did it. The dumb nurse didn't know she was talking about my sister's house. I had to come and make sure she was alright."

"Dusty has issues, but I don't think he'd...I forgot to unplug the tree. I'm sure it was just me being an idiot. I'm sure that's what caused the fire."

He squeezed her hand. "Hey, it's nothing we need to worry about right now. The fire chief will investigate what started the fire and we'll go from there. Let me talk to Chief Duncan and give him a brief update and he can have a word with Dusty." He leaned closer. "The one thing I don't want you to do is worry about anything. You never answered my question. Do you need to stay for observation?"

"I don't think so." Her grip tightened. "You're not leaving, are you?"

He smiled, so thankful to hear she didn't want him to leave. He actually wanted to leave. He wanted to find Dusty.

But he didn't trust himself. He'd hurt him if he was responsible for the fire. "I'm only going to step into the hallway to go find Chief Duncan. That's as far as I'm going."

"THANK YOU, JAMES."

He sighed. "For what?"

She looked at the doorway where Aiden had just walked out. She had to thank him as well. "For getting help finally. I miss my brother."

He sat on the edge of the bed, looking down at his lap. "It's hard to stop when I feel like my life is spinning out of control. When I heard there was a fire..." He turned his gaze to her. "I can be a jackass sometimes, but you know I love you, right?"

"I know. I love you, too."

"So...you and Officer Crowl, huh? Finally snagged the man you always wanted."

She shrugged. Had she? He said he loved her. He said he wouldn't leave her side. But she knew they had things they needed to work through.

"I still can't stand him. I didn't agree to the treatment center for him...or even you. I realized, after the shit with Dusty...I realized I needed to change for myself. I guess this is goodbye for a while, well, if they let me back in. I kinda acted like a maniac when I left."

"I'll be there for you every step of the way."

"I know." He leaned forward to kiss her forehead, then stood up. "I'm glad you're okay."

He left without another word. She figured she should be thankful for the few words they exchanged. They didn't have many brotherly-sisterly moments like they'd just had.

And *I love yous*? They rarely said that either. But in that brief time, she saw the brother she remembered from childhood, before the alcohol started to take over. She couldn't wait to see that brother all the time.

Dr. Pearson walked in to check on her and let her know she'd be discharged soon. Erin came in with a scrub shirt to change into since her shirt had been dirty and full of blood from her wound. Erin also let her borrow an extra pair of tennis shoes she had in her locker. She was so grateful for her thoughtfulness and that she happened to have an extra pair on hand that fit her. She had nothing. No shoes, since she escaped out of the house in her bare feet. No clothes. None of her jewelry supplies. Nothing. Everything she owned was burnt to a crisp.

Aiden found her sitting on the edge of the bed, waiting patiently. She had nowhere to go. She had no one else to call. She didn't even have a phone anymore. When she saw the fire and all the smoke, she didn't stop to grab anything.

He gently sat down next to her on the bed, pulling one of her hands into his.

"Sorry it took me so long."

"It's okay." She met his gaze. "What did Chief Duncan have to say?"

"He made a few phone calls. The fire chief is aware of our suspicions. Chief Duncan left to track down Dusty and ask him a few questions."

She couldn't seem to move her eyes away from his. They just stared at each other for several long moments.

"I have no home. I have nowhere to go. I lost everything."

A tiny breath left his mouth as he pulled her hand to his lap. "You have a home with me. You might have lost all your possessions, but you didn't lose everything." His breath hitched. "I didn't lose everything. Because when I saw those flames...I thought I lost everything in my life in that moment. Come home with me."

"Okay."

What else could she say? His words took her breath away. Honestly, her mind was too frazzled to have a serious conversation.

They left a few minutes later with instructions for the stitches on her arm and a bottle of painkillers. She didn't think she'd be taking any of them, but Aiden insisted just in case. She had sliced her arm pretty good. It hurt like hell when she cut herself, but it didn't fully register she cut herself until her neighbor, Chris, who found her as she ran from the side of her house, pointed it out to her. He had already called the fire department before he saw her, the sirens echoing in the distance. By the time they arrived, the fire had touched almost every part of her house. She couldn't believe she made it out alive.

"Hey, are you okay? We're home."

She looked out the window, surprised to see he was correct. They were sitting in front of his house. Aiden helped her out of Chief Duncan's vehicle that they had borrowed, since Aiden had left the house with Bentley when he heard the news. She felt sorry, a strong need to apologize for scaring him the way she had.

Or had she? They all believed Dusty started the fire. Would someone really be that cruel to her? Was Dusty that mean and vindictive?

Aiden held her hand as they walked to his front door, both of them shivering from the cold since neither had a jacket. She noticed in the hospital his shirt was dirty and torn in one spot. She didn't ask what happened, almost afraid to hear the answer. And she couldn't say why that scared her.

He opened the door without unlocking it, another thing he probably hadn't done before he left, and let her walk in first. She froze in place, her eyes gazing at the mistletoes hanging in the hallway.

The door softly clicked shut behind her. A strong pair of arms wrapped around her as his chin rested on her shoulder.

"What's this?" she whispered.

"A trail of mistletoes. Would you like to see where it ends? Will you forgive me for my asinine behavior last weekend? Will you let me love you like you deserved to be loved?"

How could she resist those words? She didn't even want to try.

"Yes."

18

Aiden didn't realize he was holding his breath waiting for her response until she whispered one simple word.

Yes.

She said yes. He almost couldn't believe it.

He turned her around in his arms and pulled her closer. "Let me lead you."

He took a few steps. She followed blindly, trusting him to walk her backwards. When he reached the first mistletoe, he stopped. His lips dropped toward hers and he kissed her as if he'd never get to kiss her again. The heat slowly built around them, warming him from his head down to the very tips of his toes.

The first kiss ended too soon, but there were plenty more to come.

"One down."

He started moving again down the hallway until he came to the next mistletoe. A bright smile lit up her face right before he kissed her again. A kiss as sweet and fierce as the first one he delivered. A kiss that poured every ounce of his love he had for her. A kiss that said he never wanted to let go.

As he led her down the hallway, stopping every few steps to kiss her under each mistletoe that he and Bentley had painstakingly made themselves, he hoped she could feel the love he had for her. He didn't want to just say it over and over that he loved her. He wanted her to feel his love as well.

When the idea came to him to make a trail of mistletoes around his house, to kiss her, to remind her of the sweet way their love started to blossom, he started on it right away. Bentley thought he was nuts when he told him the plan. He even argued with him that there'd be no way in hell he'd being doing any sort of craft to help him. Then, in the next breath, he picked up a foam white ball and started to create what the video he found on the Internet called a mistletoe kissing ball.

They followed the instructions to the T, creating fifteen different kinds of mistletoes, not just ones formed into a ball. He wanted each one to be unique and beautiful, just like Theresa. He knew Betty, the owner of the craft store, had so many questions on the tip of her tongue when he bought all the supplies earlier this morning. He didn't offer an explanation and she never had the guts to ask.

Making each one wasn't as easy as it looked in the video, but oddly enough, he enjoyed himself. He couldn't help but savor and picture the beautiful smile Theresa would produce when she saw each one. At least that's what he hoped when he made each one and then hung them around the house.

She didn't disappoint him as they walked, stopped, and kissed under each one. Her smile brightened the light inside him like a glorious star in the sky.

When he stopped at the mistletoe in the doorway of his

bathroom, he kissed her as lovingly as he had all the other times, then rested his forehead against hers.

"How about a shower...then I'll show you the last surprise."

Her eyes misted with what he thought might be tears. "Okay."

He reluctantly stepped away from her. "Hop in and I'll go find you some clothes to put on."

She nodded, the question in her eyes, yet it didn't leave her mouth. Why wasn't he going to shower with her? Why had he suddenly stopped the passion building between them as he walked her from mistletoe to mistletoe?

Simple answer.

He needed to do one more thing before they went further than a kiss. He had a plan. He wanted to stick to it, even if he felt rushed. He hadn't planned for anything to happen until tomorrow where he would've had more time to create the perfect setting. Although it was pretty damn amazing to him. He wasn't sure he wanted to change any part of this night, besides the fire and her getting hurt, of course.

She walked into the bathroom and shut the door. He grabbed her one of his old but favorite shirts for her to wear. That was it. His boxers wouldn't fit her. There was no point of even letting her try them on. He knocked once on the bathroom door before opening it. With a quick message that he left her some clothes, leaving the part out it was only a shirt, he closed the door and decided he'd take a shower of his own in the master bathroom. He tossed his shirt in the garbage can next to the sink, considering it got ripped, probably when Bentley tackled him to the ground.

He fingered the light scrape across his abdomen, thinking how much he deserved that. Bentley had been right to stop him. He had been crazed with fear, not thinking to ask someone first if she had made it out alive. He jumped in the shower and cleaned himself up as fast as he could.

He honestly couldn't imagine his life without her. If Dusty had anything to do with it, he'd...he'd what? He knew he wanted to beat the living shit out of him, but he would never touch him in that way because he wasn't about to ruin his life over that piece of shit. No. He'd let the courts handle it and push for the stiffest penalty. He was just thankful Theresa wasn't hurt.

Walking out of his master bathroom, he stopped in his tracks at the sexy picture in front of him. Theresa stood in his old college shirt that came just above her thighs. Her hair was wet and messy, but in a beautiful way. A small, almost nervous smile escaped her lips.

He wasn't fast enough to prepare the rest of his surprise. He stood with a blue towel wrapped around his waist. Both of them stood almost naked.

"I'm tired. It's been a long night. Should I sleep in anot—"

"You're sleeping with me." His voice was firm.

Didn't she understand how much he loved her? Then his mind went back to yesterday when she asked if they could be friends. He agreed but said he'd still kiss her under the mistletoe any time they stood under one. She kissed him a few minutes ago, but perhaps she still wanted to be just friends.

He forced himself to loosen his limbs and not sound so angry. "Unless you want to sleep in the spare room."

"I...I want to sleep in here. I'm..." She frowned. "I'm just confused what's going on here. About everything...is there an us?"

Two long strides and he was by her side, grasping her hands in his and guiding her to sit on the edge of the bed. His hands held hers tightly as he gazed into her eyes. "I want there to be an us. I screwed up. I got...scared." He took a deep breath.

Then it came out. Every single thing he held inside about Cynthia. The hurt, the anger, the pain. Through it all, Theresa held his hands, her eyes glued to his with concern and understanding.

"I haven't felt as happy as I do now in a long time. You bring me happiness. You fill up my darkness with light again. Please say you'll forgive my idiotic behavior and give me another chance."

She bit her lip, her eyes looking into his as if searching for something, an answer he hadn't offered yet. "I think what hurt the most was how you could ignore me after we shared something so special. It's okay if you don't want to talk. It's okay if you need time to yourself. But please don't ignore me like that again."

"Never again."

Her eyes finally turned down. "Did you mean it when you said you loved me?"

He didn't like how she pulled away from him by turning her head down. With a light nudge, he raised her chin. Her eyes were locked with his once again. "Today, tomorrow, and forever."

The sweetest, most beautiful smile touched her lips. "I love you, too."

A kiss would make this moment perfect, but he needed one more thing before he did that.

"Don't move."

He got up and walked to his closet, shuffling a box down from the top shelf. Pulling out the last mistletoe he made, he walked back to the bed, sitting down gently as he held it out to her.

Her eyes shimmered with unshed tears. "It's gorgeous."

It was a simple mistletoe, but beautiful. At least he thought so. He picked out the best one he made for this moment. Simple artificial green leaves with red holly berries mixed in. Tied on the top was a deep red bow. Not a perfect bow, but the best he could do. He was damn proud of himself for all the mistletoes he and Bentley made.

"Not as gorgeous as you. I made it myself. I made all of these hanging in my house. With some help from Bentley."

She looked surprised. "You did? You really made all of these for me?"

"I'd make a hundred more if you asked me to."

Her smile widened. "I feel like I'm seeing a whole new side of you right now. No one has ever been this sweet, kind, and loving to me."

"And I've never felt inclined to act this way. Everything I did is because I wanted to, not because I had to." He glanced at the mistletoe in her hand. "You missed something important."

Surprised again, she jerked her attention from him to the mistletoe. A lone tear slid down her cheek as soon as she saw it. Her fingers trembled as she plucked the diamond ring off one of the green leaves.

He slid off the bed to kneel on one knee as he placed his hands on her bare thighs. "It hasn't been long. Hell, I know it's crazy to even contemplate getting engaged so soon. But I know what I want. I'm damn sure of what I want." His fingers tightened on her soft thighs. "I want to spend the rest of my life with you. Will you marry me, Theresa?"

HER EMOTIONS WERE TUMBLING EVERYWHERE at the moment. Joy. Nerves. Exhilaration. Panic. Happiness. Wariness. But the one feeling overriding it all…love.

She loved him. He said he loved her. He said so many things tonight that gave her a better understanding of his attitude. This whole time she thought he was pulling away because he loved Cynthia too much to love another. Not even close. He shied away because he loved *her* so much it frightened him.

She wanted to soak up every little moment from tonight and savor it until the end of time. She had no idea he could be this sweet and romantic.

"You're making me a little nervous. Say something."

Aiden's whispered words had her smiling wide and slipping the ring on her finger.

"Yes. A thousand times, yes."

His hands slid up her thighs as he leaned forward to kiss her. It melted her on the spot. The kiss was soft and soothing, tender and sweet. His kisses always had a way of filling her heart with delight and contentment.

She felt him grab the mistletoe from her lap and a quiet thud hit the floor. Laying back as he pressed her further into the mattress, the kiss started to turn fierce and hungry. Moaning a little at the ache he was creating, she wrapped her arms tighter around him.

Breaking the kiss, his lips stayed almost pressed to hers as he whispered, "I need you. Badly. But not if it'll hurt you more."

Besides her arm that throbbed a little bit from the incision, she felt fine. A little shaken from the night, but she needed him. Just as badly. He'd soothe the shakes with his gentle kisses and smooth hands.

"I want you."

He grinned, a sweet, almost rakish grin. "Good." Lifting up some, he grabbed his towel and flung it to the floor, then removed her shirt just as easily. "Move to the center of the bed."

She scooted back until she found the middle and sighed happily when he pressed his wonderful body to hers. Small, light kisses started on her lips, making a trail down her chin, neck, then gradually up to her ear where he nibbled for a taste. The entire time she slowly rubbed her hands up and down his back in smooth, small strokes.

A kiss landed on her shoulder where the faint mark of his hickey he gave her last time showed. "Wow. I don't remember doing this."

A chuckle left her lips. "I do. It felt wonderful."

His eyes sparkled with a strong craving. "So I have permission to do it again?"

Nodding with a wily smile, she inhaled sharply as he slid down her body and his warm breath touched her most intimate spot.

"And here? Do I have permission?"

"Oh, yes."

He said nothing else but lay his soft lips down, his tongue darting out and spiraling her body into passionate bliss. Her hands fisted the comforter tightly as he stroked and licked and suckled every tiny emotion hidden inside her. His mouth just knew what spot to touch and how to touch it, she couldn't help but squirm and moan and enjoy every little sensation he pulled out of her.

It didn't take long for her to cry out with ecstasy. He moved back up her body lazily, kissing her lightly on the lips.

"You taste delicious." His hands cupped her cheeks. "Are you really mine?"

She wrapped her arms tightly around him. Her legs circled his waist with no wiggle room to escape. "I'm all yours. You can never escape."

He chuckled. "Good thing I never plan to." Brushing his mouth against hers again, his tongue ducked in briefly before he pulled away. "Can I escape for a moment to grab a condom? I'm not sure how much longer I can hold off."

She released him and he quickly darted to the bathroom and back within a few seconds. He sheathed himself and then thrust into her with happy abandon. He felt perfect and right and everything she always dreamed of.

She couldn't believe he asked her to marry him, or the wonderful surprise of all the mistletoes dangling in his house. Such a romantic gesture. Something no one had ever done for her. She liked this hidden sweet side of him. It would be impossible to walk around his house without stepping under the beautiful mistletoes he created. Which was probably his intention. So he could kiss her anytime he wanted. With a good excuse to do it.

And his kiss at the moment had her toes curling and her belly flipping and her heart soaring as he moved in and out of her like a wild stallion bucking away.

The magic in the room grew so high she swore she saw stars as another orgasm, more epic than the last one, tore through her. He followed her shortly after thrusting a few more times, then rested his heavy weight on her. She adored the feeling so much she tightened her arms around him so he couldn't move.

"I love you, Theresa. I plan to show you how much every day of our lives."

Sighing happily, with a soft kiss to his neck, she whispered, "I love you, too. I can't wait to make beautiful memories with you."

19

Theresa tried not to hesitate as they walked to the door of the diner. Aiden opened the door, allowing her to walk in first. Her feet almost stalled until he turned her in his arms and planted the sweetest, toe-curling kiss upon her lips.

With a small chuckle, his eyes turned up. "Mistletoe."

She followed his gaze and laughed as well. Above them hung the first mistletoe that brought them together with a small, chaste kiss to the cheek. They already had so many wonderful memories.

"I can sense you're nervous and I'm not sure why. Everything's going to be okay."

Appreciating his concern, she laid her head to his chest. "I'm homeless. I lost all of my belongings. And it just hurts."

"You have a home with me. And your belongings..." He sighed. "I'm sorry about that. We'll get through this. Together. I'm not leaving your side, okay?"

Lifting her head, she smiled. "Thank you."

They started to walk again, a few sets of eyes on them as she led the way with Aiden following her, his hand locked with hers. Before she could make it behind the counter, the kitchen door swung open and Bonzo's concerned face filled the space.

"Theresa, my girl!" He pulled her into the biggest, warmest hug she ever received. Almost fatherly-like. She loved it because he was about the closest thing to a father she had, considering her real father wasn't the greatest in that department. "How are you?"

He let her go. She took a step back, leaning back into the comforting body of Aiden, who must've known she needed the extra support.

"I've been better, Bonzo. I..."

"Well, butter my biscuit. Congratulations." Bonzo's eyes widened in surprise as they zoomed in on her hand that sparkled with the diamond ring.

It didn't take long for a round of congratulations from the other patrons in the diner to circle them. A few regulars that came every Sunday for brunch and Mrs. Wayworth.

"Oh, that is a stunning ring. You're a lucky man, Aiden, for snatching up this wonderful lady." Mrs. Wayworth winked at him as Theresa slightly blushed at the compliment.

"I am the luckiest. There's no way I was letting her get away."

She patted his arm. "Well, it's good to see you happy again. And that handsome smile of yours." Then Mrs. Wayworth turned her attention to Theresa. "My sister received her Christmas present in the mail, and boy, I chided her for it, but she opened it already and loved the necklace. Absolutely loved it. I gave her your number because she wouldn't let it go until I did. I do believe you'll have more orders soon."

Theresa wanted to smile at that, and she did somewhat. But she had no idea how she could make any kind of jewelry anytime soon. All her supplies were destroyed in the fire. Even her phone. She couldn't take any phone calls until she bought a new one.

Maybe Mrs. Wayworth saw all of those harrowing emotions on her face because she smiled tenderly. "I'm sorry to hear about the fire last night. I'm so glad you made it out safely."

"Thank you, Mrs. Wayworth. I'm very happy to hear your sister liked the necklace. Please tell her it might be a few days before I can return any phone calls. My phone was destroyed, along with all my jewelry supplies."

"I'll let her know. Don't you worry about a thing, Theresa dear. Everything always has a way of working out."

Mrs. Wayworth said a few more encouraging words and then went back to her meal.

"Come on." Bonzo gestured his head to follow him to the kitchen.

Aiden grabbed her hand and ventured to the kitchen with her. Bonzo set a small box on the counter near the door and smiled.

"Mrs. Johnson was in here earlier, picking up her jewelry order. Sure am glad you kept your inventory here. It would've been a shame to lose all that hard work making all these beautiful presents for people. What can I do to help you, Theresa?"

Tears started to form in the corners of her eyes at the kindness shimmering back at her. "I have no idea. This is all new to me. I feel like I'm starting all over."

"Well, you just let me know what you need and I'm there. Take a few days off."

"Oh, no, I can't do that, Bonzo. I need the money."

Aiden wrapped his arms around her and squeezed tightly as he laid a kiss to the side of her head. "If you need a few days for yourself, take it. I don't want you to worry about money. I'll take care of you."

Bonzo's eyes twinkled with delight. "What he said. Let someone take care of you for once. You work too hard. You deserve it." He tossed a hand to the box. "You didn't even need to come in for this today. I would've handed them out."

She wiped a stray tear from her eye. "I appreciate that, Bonzo. I'd like to make sure everyone gets their order. I'll be at work tomorrow." Tensing slightly, she gasped. "How am I going to get to work? I always walked and now—"

Aiden swiftly turned her around and cupped her cheeks lightly as he pressed a gentle kiss to her lips. "I'll drive you. You can borrow my car. We'll buy you a car. It doesn't matter how you'll get to work, because you will. We'll figure this out. Together. Maybe I'm suddenly coming on strong, but I never want you to doubt how I feel about you again."

Her breathing, that had skyrocketed when she panicked, gradually returned to normal as he laid a few more delicate kisses to her lips.

"We're in this together, right, Theresa?"

"Yes," she whispered breathlessly.

Oh, they were so in this together. He had been her rock all night, loving her passionately and without restraint. This morning when she woke up in a panic, last night's events rushing through her mind, Aiden had been there to calm her down, telling her everything would be all right. She believed it would be. Because they'd be together. His strength would help keep hers together when all she felt like doing was falling apart because she had lost everything.

"I can still hand these out. Leave them here. You worry about you. There's no sense in going around dropping these off." She turned around, Aiden's arms still holding her together as she looked at Bonzo as he continued. "You never planned to go deliver them house to house. Why change the plan? You let them come to the diner to pick these up."

How could she explain the sudden need to make sure everyone got their Christmas gifts? The fire, the loss of everything she owned, it burned a hole in her gut the entire morning until she finally told Aiden she had to go to the diner and pick up her jewelry and deliver it, not wait for the people to come to the diner. Maybe she just wanted to make sure they all had a wonderful Christmas when she wasn't sure she would. How could she believe she would when she didn't even have a proper change of clothes? Right now she was wearing one of Aiden's shirts and a pair of sweats that she had to tie tightly so they wouldn't fall down, and one of his large winter coats that almost made her look like a drowned rat. She had to look ridiculous, yet every time he glanced her way, she felt like the most beautiful woman on Earth.

"I..." She hesitated. The words wouldn't come, the explanation still difficult. Okay, maybe it was a silly thing to worry about. "Okay. Thanks, Bonzo."

She wouldn't worry about it. At least she completed all of her orders and brought them to work before the fire wiped out every single thing she owned in one swift move.

"Go home. Let Aiden take care of you. Just relax. If you want to come in tomorrow, then I'd love to see you. If not, you don't worry about a thing."

She hugged Bonzo in response, said a quick hi to Shelly, his wife, and left. As she buckled her seatbelt, the nerves she experienced back in the diner came rushing back. What was she going to do? How was she going to replace all of her possessions? The supplies for her jewelry weren't cheap. Clothing could get so expensive. Everything felt like a huge weight on her shoulders.

A warm hand enveloped hers. "Look at me, sweetheart."

Her eyes glided to his.

"It's going to be the best damn Christmas this year. You know how I know? Because I get to spend it with you. That's what matters right now. Everything else, well, we'll figure it out." He pulled her hand to his lips and kissed it. "I love you."

When he said it that way, she believed him. Everything would work out.

"I love you, too."

THE DOORBELL RANG.

"I'll get it," Aiden hollered as he walked out of the kitchen.

He figured Theresa assumed he'd get it, especially since she'd been engrossed in arranging her jewelry in just the right way. She said there was a certain order she liked all of her pieces to be organized.

They were both surprised when the doorbell rang the first time, soon after they arrived home from the diner. Standing with a sweet smile, Betty from the craft store had a whole bag of goodies. So many supplies to fill up a new jewelry box that Theresa had adamantly insisted Betty take it back. Betty wouldn't hear any of it. She insisted Theresa take it all and make her a beautiful necklace in thanks. That's all she wanted.

Shortly after Betty left, Daphne showed up with some clothes. The light in Theresa's eyes at the sight of everything made tears form, almost in Aiden's eyes as well.

Person after person after person stopped by, dropping things off for her. Crazy things from wonky looking

Christmas decorations they thought she'd like, to practical things like a brush and hair accessories.

He knew the town could get into everyone's business on occasion, rumors spreading, gossip running rampant. But he'd never seen people come together in such a beautiful way. Theresa lost everything she owned in the fire last night. Now his house was so full of things, it's as if they had packed up her house and moved her in.

The town had come forward to make Theresa feel loved and happy and that everything was going to be okay. Just as he had told her repeatedly today, even as he said it, wondering if it really would be. He hated seeing the pain and sadness in her eyes. A few times it made him nervous he wouldn't be able to remove it all on his own. And he didn't. The entire town helped him, and he couldn't be more grateful.

Pulling open the door, he smiled at Chief Duncan, Lynn, Laura, Gregory, and Gabby, who all stood on his porch, their arms full of things he wasn't sure where he'd put.

"We've come bearing gifts," Chief Duncan said with merry, leaning in a bit closer to him, "and some news."

Aiden nodded, anxious to hear what he had to say. "Come on in. Theresa's in the living room sorting her jewelry and in heaven at all the beads. You guys are too kind to bring more stuff."

"It's just terrible what happened. We don't mind helping out." Lynn glided by him with Laura right behind her.

He winked at Laura. "Hey, pipsqueak."

She blushed and giggled. "Hey."

"We thought you might be busy and overwhelmed, so Gabby brought some fixings for a delicious roast dinner. We'll go get that started." Gregory smiled wide as he followed Gabby, who had a large pan in her hands.

Aiden closed the door, then turned to Chief Duncan, the only one left in the hallway. "I hope this is news I'll enjoy hearing."

The chief grinned and nodded as he set the box he was holding to the floor. "This is just some kitchen stuff Lynn thought Theresa would need." His eyes sparkled with mischief. "Maybe you already have them stocked yourself. I hear congratulations are in order. I'm happy you two worked things out."

"Because of you. Thanks for helping me get my head out of my ass. Last night...if I would've lost her..."

Chief Duncan squeezed his shoulder. "But you didn't. We didn't."

Aiden steeled his spine, not wanting to cry in front of the chief, even though the tears threatened to flow. He almost lost the woman he loved in a brutal fire. He hated thinking about it. Of course, it was difficult to erase last night's events with the reminder every time someone stopped by with more gifts.

"So, the news?"

Chief Duncan nodded. "We found Dusty earlier this morning sleeping in his car on the outskirts of Mason. Pretty sure he was sleeping off a drunken night. Fire Chief Monroe hasn't completed his investigation yet, but there are signs it was started deliberately. It didn't take long, with a little prodding, for Dusty to confess to starting the fire."

Aiden shook his head. "This will put Theresa at ease that she wasn't at fault, because it bothered her that she might've been. But damn, now it makes it my fault."

"How so?"

"I might've told him to stay the hell away from her or else...right before you hauled him away the night of the bar fight."

Chief Duncan waved his hand carelessly in the air. "It's not your fault either. Dusty's a loose cannon. How about you two focus on your upcoming nuptials and put all this behind you. Just have a merry Christmas."

"I plan to have the best damn Christmas I've ever had."

He didn't doubt it for one second. With Theresa by his side, Christmas couldn't get any better.

The evening went by quickly, the house full of loud laughter and happiness. It was the first time he had ever had a little gathering at his house. He liked the picture in front of him, of the beautiful merriment ringing.

Theresa finally looked at ease and the worry gone, especially when he whispered to her Dusty was the cause of the fire. She had tensed at first, then slowly smiled, obviously relieved she wasn't the cause because she constantly forgot to unplug the Christmas tree. She told him firmly he had to double check the tree was unplugged before they went to bed every night. He smiled, kissed her, and assured her he'd take the responsibility of that task.

By the time they finished the wonderful roast Gabby cooked, ate a piece of pie Lynn had baked, and played a board game picked by Laura, the sun had descended and the stars twinkled brightly in the sky. Everyone left, and they finally had the house to themselves.

Aiden made a fire, plugged in the Christmas tree, and pulled Theresa into his arms to the floor.

"What a day, huh?"

She nodded, resting her head against his chest as he wrapped his arms around her, tucking her into his body.

"You feeling okay?"

"I feel wonderful. I feel grateful for such wonderful friends. I have no words."

He kissed the top of her head as the fire crackled and the

tree lit up with delight before them. "I was surprised myself. But it just shows how much everyone cares about you. See, I said it would all work out."

"Do you want to know what my favorite part of everything that happened today is?"

"Of course."

She inhaled deeply, snuggling more comfortably into his arms. "This. Sitting here with you. It just makes me feel... happy."

She made him feel the same. Just happy. Content. As if everything in his world was good, bright, and merry. She took the darkness filling him up inside and washed it away with her lightness.

"You are my happiness, Theresa."

EPILOGUE

CHRISTMAS MORNING

UNDERNEATH THE CHRISTMAS tree wasn't brimming with loads of presents. Only two, in fact. One for him. One for her. He couldn't wait for Theresa to open the gift he bought her. When he first pulled it off the shelf, he hesitated. Would she think it silly? Would she find it offensive? Would she grace him with the sweet smile he loved?

Well, he was about to find out.

"Open mine first."

Or not. Guess she wanted him to open the present from her first.

He gently took the gift from her outstretched hand. Even though they only had these two gifts, they sat in front of the tree as if they had a mountain of gifts to open. Oh, and there'd be plenty of gifts to open later. They planned to celebrate Christmas with his parents after lunch. Theresa had no idea there were gifts waiting for her. He wanted to surprise her.

While she appreciated people in town coming to her

rescue and giving her things she needed instead of draining her savings to buy it, she didn't want anything else. She didn't want to be the center of attention.

Because she was such a sweet and generous woman, she created a beautiful piece of jewelry for each person that stopped by bearing gifts. She wanted to show her thanks with more than just simple words.

Yesterday had been a very long day. They dropped off each gift, saying thanks and receiving hugs, thank yous, and so many Merry Christmases he almost got Christmased out. Was that even possible?

She worked hard each night stringing beads, tying knots, and organizing each piece of jewelry into something magical. Of course, he sat next to her helping as best as he could. Not because he felt like he had to. Because he wanted to. He loved the joy that filled each facet of her face when he first offered. Anytime he could elicit that sweet sensation out of her, he'd do whatever it took.

He even pulled some strings so she could see her brother, which she had yesterday. Normally visitors weren't allowed, and with his behavior the night of the fire, they almost didn't let him back into the program. They also wanted to slap charges on him. After a few kind words from Chief Duncan, Aiden asking him graciously to do it, for Theresa's sake, of course, they decided not to press charges for him hitting the security guard.

Her brother looked good, ragged but good, like the program was tough and tiring, but working. He had a long road ahead of him. Theresa would be there to help him, as would he. Only for Theresa's sake. Because he still didn't like James. Just as James didn't like him. Although they were cordial only because neither wanted to upset Theresa.

"Open it. You're killing me here."

He chuckled, swiped a kiss, and pushed all other thoughts out of his mind as he tore open the present. Brushing the white tissue paper aside, he couldn't hold back the laughter as he pulled out a red mug with the sweetest saying written in bold white letters around it. *Give me a kiss, I'll give you a coffee.*

"Is this your way of telling me I don't get my daily coffee unless I give you a kiss?"

She smirked in the most adorable way. "Maybe." Her eyes shifted down, a light red blush coating her cheeks. "I wasn't sure what to get you. It's been so crazy these past few weeks with...everything. I saw that and it just said *buy me!* So I did."

Wrapping a tender hand around the back of her neck, he pulled her closer for a kiss. Light and tender. Because anything more passionate would've had him carrying her back to the bedroom for a different kind of Christmas fun.

Pulling away slightly, his mouth still close to hers, he whispered, "It's the best damn present I've ever gotten. I'm going to use it every day." He chuckled, pressing his lips to hers. "I can't wait for you to open your present."

She shifted away, the reluctance in her eyes almost saying she wanted to go back to the bedroom like him, but instead she picked up the gift he bought her.

Biting her lip, she took her time unwrapping the paper around the box, then her eyes widened in surprise as she broke into a bout of laughter that was contagious. His middle almost hurt as they laughed together, the loud noise ringing around the room, filling it with so much happiness he was surprised he didn't burst from it all.

Sitting on her lap in all its glory was a top-of-the-line coffee maker.

He planned to teach his beautiful, wonderful fiancé how

to make a delicious cup of coffee. Even if he failed, he'd stop at the diner every day before his shift with his new coffee mug and get one of her cups of coffee. Because no matter how horrible it tasted, he knew she made it with love. He didn't doubt that for one second. Because why else would he keep going into the diner, day after day, paying for a cup of coffee that never slid down his throat with delight?

Because he probably loved her for a long time and was just too afraid to admit it. Not anymore.

"This is the perfect present."

"Goes well with mine." He lifted his mug.

They started to laugh as if it was the funniest joke of the century. He didn't care if it wasn't that funny. It felt good to laugh again. It felt good to be happy. To be in love.

He set the cup aside, took the coffee maker from her lap, and slid over her body, making her drop gently to the floor so she was flat on her back.

"I don't think I can make it to the bedroom. I'm going to love you right here. In front of this gorgeous Christmas tree."

She brushed a lock of his dark brown hair back. "Sounds like a beautiful memory to make."

His lips found hers.

The moment turned into a memory they would never forget.

DON'T MISS THE NEXT BOOK IN THIS HEARTWARMING HOLIDAY SERIES!

CHRISTMAS WISH

FOR BENTLEY & EMMA'S STORY
CHRISTMAS WISH
A HOLIDAY ROMANCE NOVEL, #3

What if you had one wish granted for Christmas? What would it be?

Acting reckless isn't something Bentley Wilson is known for, but when he runs back into a burning building to save a little girl's puppy after specifically told not to do so, that's exactly how most of the town sees him, especially the fire chief who insists he has to help with the annual Christmas party because of his behavior. Throw in the fact the woman he's pined over for too long is getting married, this holiday is going to go down as one of the worst. Until he meets Emma Brookes. She's feisty, headstrong, and holds so much pain hidden in the depths of her beautiful green eyes. He wants nothing more than to erase her sadness. But it's already a season of disaster, and every time they're together, they spar like two warriors dueling to the death. Despite that, he likes the challenge, the crazy way she makes him feel. Before the holiday is over, he vows to get his one Christmas wish. That she never leaves his side.

FOR JAMES & ERIN'S STORY
SNOWED IN LOVE
A HOLIDAY ROMANCE NOVEL, #4

A blizzard. A cabin. A cup of hot chocolate.
The perfect mixture to fall in love.

James Brennen is nothing but a screwup. At least, in the small town of Mulberry, that's what everyone thinks of him. As a recovering alcoholic, he's trying his best to turn his life around, to be a better man. All of his hard work comes crashing down when he's fired from his job at the hospital— accused of stealing drugs. Nothing ever changes and he's done trying to prove himself. Needing time alone, his friend's cabin in the middle of the woods provides the perfect escape. He knows he's found deep trouble, not only when he gets stranded during a brutal snowstorm, but that he's stuck with the one woman he's wanted since the first day he laid eyes on her. The passion burns bright between them, but it doesn't matter, because as soon as Christmas is over, he's leaving for good.

FOR STU & CHASITY'S STORY
SNOWFLAKES AND SHOTS
A HOLIDAY ROMANCE NOVEL, #5

One last shot at love...

Stu doesn't have many regrets in life—not even the fact he never decorates his bar for the holidays. But when a bar fight turns into needing medical attention, he's put face-to-face with the one woman he's tried to avoid for the last fifteen years. Okay, so maybe he regrets a few things. He should've never walked away from her. It only took a good knock to his head to make him see clearly. He's going to win Chasity's heart once again. It doesn't matter that she's not going to make it easy; he's up for the challenge. Bring on the bets and all the Christmas spirit he can handle. Except, one person doesn't like the idea of them together—the same person that had him walking away from her all those years ago.

FOR MASE & HOPE'S STORY
HOLIDAY HOPE
A HOLIDAY ROMANCE NOVEL, #6

Let the merriment begin...Operation Holiday Hope commence.

Life hasn't been the same since she quit her job working for the tyrant mayor, but Hope Bronson is trying her best. She's attempting to embrace the holiday spirit and pretend she's happy when, in reality, she feels stuck in a rut. And why? She can't even explain it to herself, let alone to anyone else, without risking being called a drama queen. And men... don't even get her started. Talk about bad choices every. Single. Time. Except...maybe one guy, but she can't trust her own judgment. It doesn't matter that everyone tells her he's a good one. She's leery of opening herself up to another bad decision—unless he can convince her otherwise.

Mase Brandt can't believe his luck when he's asked to fix a Nativity scene for the church. The one and only woman to steal his heart with ease works there. A few months ago, she shut him out with little fanfare. This time, he's not giving up so easily. The holidays are a joyous time of year. He'll use anything and everything to his advantage to win her heart. He knows she won't make a moment of it easy on him. But that's okay. He has a few tricks up his sleeve. Let the festivities begin.

For Cam & Serenity's Story
Sleigh All the Way
A Holiday Romance Novel, #7

There's no such thing as too much holiday cheer...right?

If there's one thing Cam is good at, it's working with his hands. So making a sleigh for the woman who loves Christmas with a passion seems like a foolproof plan to win her heart. He's done being stuck in the friend zone. Except he's a little rusty with dating. After keeping women at a distance for so long, he's going to need more help than he realized. Who knew he'd get it from where he least expected it—her twin boys. This should be easy-peasy. But one thing Cam has learned: nothing ever works out like he plans.

Serenity doesn't like it known, but she hates Christmas. With a passion. The last thing she can do is let anyone know, especially her boys. She'd never ruin the holiday for them. Besides faking holiday cheer, she finds herself having to resist the one man who is impossible to resist. Cam is everything she always wanted in a guy: kind, caring, always there for her when she needs him. But they're friends, and losing him from her life can't happen. Venturing into the sex-zone would ruin it all. If there is one thing she's good at, it's pretending. All she has to do is make him believe being friends is for the best.

ABOUT THE AUTHOR

I'm a *USA Today* Bestselling Author that loves to write contemporary romance and romantic suspense novels, although I am partial to romantic suspense. I even dabble in paranormal. Honestly, I love anything that has to do with romance. As long as there's a happy ending, I'm a happy camper. And insta-love...yes, please! I love baseball (Go Twins!) and creating awesome crafts. I graduated with a Bachelor's Degree in Criminal Justice, working in that field for several years before I became a stay-at-home mom. I have a few more amazing stories in the works. If you would like to learn more about me and my books, head to my website by scanning the QR code. Thanks for reading!

Scan me